Murdoc

The Princes of Arcadia

K. L. STEPHENS

Karen L. Stephens

Contents

Copyright

Copyright © K. L. Stephens 2023

This is a work of fiction, Names, characters, places, and incidents either are the product of the author's imagination or are used fictitiously. Any resemblance to actual persons, living or dead, events or locales is entirely coincidental.

All rights reserved: No part of this book may be reproduced or used in any manner without written permission of the copyright owner except for the use of quotations in a book review.

Printed in the United States of America

First E-Book published: 2023

Cover Photos Supplied by: Shutterstock

Dedication

To my beautiful daughters, Kristine, and Sara.
You both are the light of my life and the joy in my heart.

Intorduction

Prejudice is Not Only a Human Emotion

Murdoc

I am one of the six Princes of Arcadia, four hundred years old, and the longing to mate is strong. Now I have found my mate. But prejudices within my clan may make it impossible for me to claim her. Members of my clan hate humans. They believe I should choose a mate among Lycan high born or not mate at all. My mate is human, or so I thought. There are dangers surrounding her, and what she is, can I claim my mate and keep her safe from members of my clan?

Melissa

Finally, I befriended the Lycans that have a compound outside the city where I live and work as a doctor. None of them have suspected what I truly am. Nearly a thousand years ago, my forebearer grandmother a witch mated to a Lycan in the mountains of Germany, in her visions she cast a spell on me, suppressing my powers, and laying my Lycan side dormant until I am found and claimed by my mate. Living my short life among humans until he showed up. Murdoc, a Prince of Arcadia, and the Leader of Clan Sinclair has awakened my powers and beast. Then he left. I have had visions of the dangers both he and I are facing but his life is in danger. Should I follow and save him? Or just go back to my dormant side?

Prologue

High in the Mountains of Germany
1525

Esmee

The babe was not going to come, just as I had seen in my visions. I will die here in the bed that Martio, my Lycan mate, has shared for two hundred years. When I turned my head and squinted out the door, he listened to the midwife as she spoke softly. I felt no fear of what was going to come, I had been prepared for this. Martio grew as his Lycan came forth, reaching out my hand, "Martio," my voice was not much more than a raspy whisper. But he heard me.

He slowly knelt near our bed, "You must regain your strength, then bring the babe forth." His voice quivered as a tear slid down his face, reaching out his hand to stroke my face, and pushing back my sweat-drenched hair.

Nearly too weak to even smile, "The babe and I will be with the goddess soon, my love." I whispered, trying desperately to raise my hand to wipe away his tears.

Martio took my hand and brought it to his mouth kissing the inside of my wrist and then my palm, he uttered, "I never should have let you wander out in the woods alone when you were carrying the babe."

"Shh, this is not your fault." I said, "I had to protect her. You know that." I tried to explain again. "I had seen that this would be my last babe, and we would join the goddess in the great beyond." Closing my eyes for just a moment to gain the strength to tell him all of it. "All of our granddaughters for nearly a thousand years will perish, there will be Lycans that will hunt them. I had to protect her, she is the last of my line, and will be powerful, even more, powerful than me."

"What will I do without you?" his voice trailed off.

There was a shiver of light that only I could see, the goddess was coming for us. My life was slipping away, and I had to tell him what I had done. "It does not matter now." Taking another shaky breath, I needed to finish, "Martio, one day, many years from now, we will have a powerful witch as a granddaughter. I cast a spell on her binding her powers and lying dormant her Lycan side, to protect her. A powerful Lycan will come to claim her and awaken her." Tears were streaming down his face, and I could tell he did not understand, "I saw so many threats to her, I cast the spell to keep her safe. Until she finds and only when she finds her fated mate."

"Why are you telling me this?" He muttered.

"Because you must know, this is why I am laying here now." Taking a deep breath, it was getting harder and harder to hold on. "I gave my life and the life of our babe for the life of our so many great-granddaughters, that she may live." I could see the goddess now standing in the corner, she held my unborn baby in her arms, reaching out her hand for me to join them so that we could travel to the hereafter. With my last breath, "I will be waiting for you, my love. Please forgive me." Closing my eyes, I felt my life leave my body, then just as my lifeless body let out my last death rattle. Now I stood beside the goddess cradling my sweet babe in my arms watching as my mate lowered his head and wept still holding my lifeless hand in his.

"Martio will live a long time to come." The goddess said, "But you will be with him at the end."

In the centuries to come the prediction Esmee made came true all the females of her line perished at hands of Lycan witch hunters. Now, Doctor Melissa Herbert, the last of Esmée's line was already in hiding when a Lycan killed her parents ten years ago, she has not been found. She still lives as a human, until she meets Murdoc.

Chapter 1

Woods Outside Sinclair Castle
Present Day

Murdoc

Dusk was upon us, as I stood back from the line of trees looking at the remains of Sinclair castle, I was a mere pup of three in 1600 when the blast destroyed it, but my father told me about it. The noise was deafening, and the earth shook for miles around. When they ran and watched as much of the tower fell to the ground, burying members of the human Sinclair clan underneath.

MacDonald, my commander walked up behind me. "The sentries are all posted, and have been given their orders, your highness." Bowing his head to me, after he gave his report. Normally I am not out here, but for some reason, tonight I felt like looking at the castle.

"I don't remember what it looked like before," I nodded toward the castle, humans were walking around taking pictures of the ruins. "Now it is just a page in the human history books. Most don't want to even travel this far north to see it." I muttered.

As I looked at the ghostly shell of the tower and castle ruins, I felt a twinge of sadness that the humans had never rebuilt. Now centuries later, they were still battling in the human courts over the title and land, and no longer on the fields that surrounded the castle. The land and castle that I considered more mine than any humans. We were the ones that guarded it. Glazing up to a third-floor window, there in that windowsill was the clue to the treasure my brother helps to guard. And until my brother or one of his friends came to retrieve it, I would make sure my sentries stand watch.

I turned toward my commander, "Let's head back, it will be dark soon, and the humans will leave." There were fewer and fewer tourists each passing year that ventured to the castle.

"Humans," he scoffed, "You should just put up a barrier to keep those retched humans out."

"And when the human government came to investigate, what would we do then?" It was a rhetorical question.

"Kill them all," He grumbled, "Humans do not have any place in this world. Look what they have done to it." He continued. "But I guess they are better than any witches that used to plague the earth."

I stopped in my tracks, "Witches? You hate them as well?" I was trying to lighten his mood, but I could see the seriousness on his face. MacDonald was a good and stern commander, but his hatred of other beings in our world was common knowledge in my clan. Ignoring it for the most part, because he was a long-time friend, but I knew one day his hatred was going to get him into some serious trouble.

As if he had read my thoughts, he took a deep breath and asked. "Have you heard from your brother?"

I smiled, "Lucas is mated, and they had a son." Unconsciously I looked up to the sky, even with the sun still up I knew that another full moon was going to pass me by, and the urge to mate, stronger and stronger with each one.

Glancing over my shoulder I saw the disgruntled look on my commander's face, "What?" I grumbled.

"I didn't say anything," looking guilty.

Stopping on the trail turning to face him, "I can see the look on your face. What is on your mind?" I demanded.

With a sigh, "Why don't you just choose a mate among the high-born females? I am sure any of them and their families would be honored to have a Prince of Arcadia as a mate."

"You sound like a broken record," I grumbled, "Every full moon for the last one hundred years, you have spouted the same thing."

Shaking his head, "It isn't just me, that thinks you should mate to a Lycan high-born. Many of the elders of the clan believe so too." He stood his ground, "You are a Prince of Arcadia, gods forbid that your mate should be some lowly human." He turned his head and spit, an insult to the thought that my mate would be human.

Not about to get back into his conversation, I continued walking and called over my shoulder. "Your prejudice will get you into trouble one day, my friend,"

"Humans do not deserve to walk this earth; Lycans should be the ones to dominate," He grumbled, not letting go of the subject.

Stopping I turned and grew, "Quelch this hatred now!" I growled low. "I am the Prince of Arcadia, not you or any other member of this clan. When and only when I find my fated mate, human or otherwise, I will be proud to have her as my mate. And if my mate turns out to be human or any other being, you will treat her with the respect she will be due as my mate. And address her as Your Highness just as you do me. Understood?"

"Your Highness." He bowed. I could not understand his hatred toward others in our world. MacDonald has humans in his family tree, and his mother was human. And as far as I knew he or any of his kin had not been harmed by any other being.

Even young, he harbored this hatred and would push me to train harder. Whispering that we should go out hunting for those he considered inferior to us. My father sensed my wanting to fight, but he never knew of Macdonald's blood lust for other beings. One day, my father found me walking along this same path, when he pointed out, "Your brother has his duty, son. And you have yours, remember that." Slapping me on the back, "It was not an easy decision to put both you and your brother in the situations that you will inherit. But the council was right, being both Prince of Arcadia and one of the Knights entrusted to guard the treasure, is not easy for only one Lycan, I should know." We continued to walk back to our compound. "Neither of you will have an easy life, and I only hope one day you both will find a mate as wonderful as your mother."

My father was hard as nails, and this speech touched me, from that day forward, I took my duty seriously, I was the future Prince of Arcadia. "I know," bowing to my father.

He slapped me on the back, "I have a surprise for you, come on." We walked to the training fields, "You will start training this afternoon with these experts. You can fight, but you will learn like your brother to fight like the best." Then he stood back and watched as I trained daily. That was the end of MacDonald's pushing me.

Then, on a day much like this in 1690, my father asked me to join him on a walk, as we strode toward the castle, "It is time you inherited your title, Murdoc." My father spoke.

"Father?" I questioned.

"The treasure must be moved to a safer place. Your brother is now a knight and time for you to inherit your title." He stood with his legs braced apart, the image of my grandfather.

"I should not inherit for a long time to come," I argued.

He smiled, "You will do as you are told, and accept your duty as my heir." Even with the smile, I felt the weight of his command. "We are leaving for the new world, and there is no telling what will happen on the journey."

I nodded, accepting what he ordered, "When will you leave?"

"Once the others have gathered, and we retrieve the treasure then we will leave." Turning to me, "A member of the high council will be here with the documents to turn over the title to you before we go." With that, he turned and walked back to our home. Stopping only for a moment to turn back to me, bowing, "Your Highness."

Within a week, I was named Prince Murdoc Keithen Sinclair, Prince of Arcadia, and Laird of the Lycan Clan Sinclair.

Chapter 2

After I graduated from medical school, I applied to Mercy Hospital for my residency and was accepted. I didn't know a soul here in this city, but I was one step closer to my goal, finding my mate. My guardian angel as I call her, Esmee told me to come here, he would be here. Once I arrived, I heard rumors of a group of men living out at the old mine. I was certain they were Lycans. And I knew my mate was a powerful Lycan.

They weren't exactly the sociable type, then neither was I. That left me with a dilemma of how to get close to them. In the back of my mind, I feared them as well, though I was part Lycan myself, I was the last of a long line of powerful witches. Esmee my forbearer, cast a spell on me over a thousand years ago hiding my powers and laying my Lycan side dormant. Then like all the females in Esmée's line my parents were killed ten years ago while I was in medical school by a Lycan.

My mother and father insisted that I attend school under an alias, they had been warned of the dangers if my mother ever used her powers. But she had, and they were found, I had been visiting during a school break and had just walked out of the house when I heard my mother's screams. Father roared at the one that had set fire to his mate, but that roar didn't last long. He too was dead. Standing back in the shadows, I saw the Lycan that came out of the house I grew up in, now engulfed in flames. He looked around smelling the air, trying to find me.

Esmee spoke to me, "*You must leave Melissa. They are dead. You are all that remains.*" But I didn't leave immediately, I just watched. He didn't catch my scent, that was probably because of the charm my mother had put on me so that I would not smell like a witch. We knew a Lycan witch hunter was getting close, so my mother placed a charm on me, and because of that charm, they were found. But I saw him, and I will never forget his face, the one that killed my parents.

For the last nine years, I have blamed myself for their death, but I did as they would have wanted and continued in pursuit of becoming a surgeon. But here I was, in the city where a pack of Lycans resided not a few miles from where I lived and worked. A pack of Lycans I longed to meet and feared it all the same. The only thing I had was Esmee telling me this is where I needed to be. So, I stayed.

My life was not glamorous, I worked long and hard. Got through my residency and my fellowship. Finally, I was a full-fledged doctor, but no closer to finding my mate. Some nights when I would collapse in my bed from exhaustion, I thought about leaving. I had offers from hospitals around the country. If I did not meet my mate and be claimed, I continued to be safe. Esmee had other things to say about those thoughts, she was very adamant about it. At night in my dreams, she would show me the Lycans that were so close, told me about their grandfathers, and how she came to know them. I almost felt like I was a part of their family. So, I waited for the day I would meet the pack of Lycans and my mate.

Chapter 3

Highlands of Scotland

Murdoc

There was a knock on my study door, "Enter," I called out from the chair I occupied.

MacDonald stepped in, bowing his head, then said, "One of the sentries just reported your brother is in the forest, with a human female." There was a sneer at the end of MacDonald's report.

"Is that all?" my eyebrow shot up an inch at the hatred in his voice.

"The sentry said that he claimed her to be his." Again, he could not mask the hatred in his voice that my brother would claim a human.

Standing, I walked over to my desk and laid the book I had been reading down.

"I was not aware that you had given him permission to be on your lands," my commander grumbled.

"MacDonald, I knew my brother was here in Scotland," I said. Walking past him I continued, "Grayson is my brother, he grew up on these lands, and will always be welcome any time with or without my permission."

I didn't want to get into another discussion about his feelings regarding humans. I have had enough of them over the years. Between him and a few of the elders in my clan, it was getting harder and harder to quelch this hatred they had. Patting him on the back as I stepped through the threshold of the door, "I am going to bed. Wake me if there is any Serious trouble."

Two days later the call I received did not make my day. Looking down at my cell I saw Lucas' name on the screen. "Lucas, what happened?"

"Good afternoon, your Highness." He chuckled on the other end. "But I do have to let you know Grayson was shot yesterday outside Edinburgh University Library."

A scoff escaped my throat, "Shot, so?"

Lucas sighed, "The bullet got stuck in his clavicle, he couldn't expel it. They flew to Fergus's compound where they dug it out of the bone. He is healing now."

Lowering my head, I should have known that Lucas would not have called me if it was not important, "Thank you, Lucas." Then a thought came to me, "What was he doing in Edinburgh?"

Lucas chuckled on the other end, "I know you are a Prince, Murdoc, but you know I cannot discuss our missions even with you."

Sighing again, "I understand. And Lucas, again thank you for calling."

It was almost as if I saw him bow his head, "Your Highness." Then we disconnected the call.

Chapter 4

Melissa

"He's coming!" The French-accented woman's voice shouted startling me awake. Groaning, I lifted my arm and looked at my watch, for only an hour. That is how long I got to sleep. Closing my eyes for a moment, I knew who woke me up, she had come to me in my dreams throughout my life, warning me of dangers or things to come. Esmee, my I don't even know how many great-grandmothers she was. She explained I was the last of her line, and when I was claimed by my powerful Lycan mate, I would be even more powerful than her.

Grumbling, I spoke to the empty room, "Esmee, an hour! Could you not have given me a little longer to sleep?" No longer a resident, but these twenty-four-hour shifts at the hospital were still killer. Swinging my legs over the side of the bed I was in, I stood and stretched for a few minutes before I walked out into the hallway of the Emergency Room. I pulled my mass of hair down and ran my fingers through it before putting it back on top of my head in a bun.

There was a commotion in the emergency room, two huge men carried an elderly gentleman in, unconscious. He looked to have been beaten and had a huge lump on his head. When I got closer, I sniffed. My eyes widened, *Lycans!*

One caught my reaction, and asked, "Are you a surgeon?"

Still dumbstruck, all I could do is nod, clasping his large hand around my wrist, he growled "I have one." To his friend in what I knew to be an ancient dialect of Gaelic. Then he pulled me out of the double doors looking around to an ambulance, "Get in."

He didn't know that I knew what a Lycan is, or capable of, but I wasn't going to argue. Lycans could be dangerous, I should know, one killed my parents. But I also knew my mate was a Lycan, so I stepped up into the back of the ambulance, and after he closed the doors, I saw him get in the driver's seat and hot-wire the vehicle. Taking off, out of the hospital parking lot I called out, "Where are you taking me?"

My capture didn't bother to answer me, just kept driving. He continued to drive past the city limits and kept driving. Closing my eyes, "Emsee, keep watch over me." I whispered.

His eyes flashed red when he glanced back in the rearview mirror hearing my plea when Emsee said in my head, *They will not hurt you.* For some reason that calmed me down, Esmee had never let me down, and I believed her, so I sat back and let him drive.

As he turned up an old mine road, we climbed a hill passing old, dilapidated buildings until he stopped in front of a modern house, that was in a circle with five others. Each is different. After getting out of the driver's side, he moved around to the back of the ambulance opening the doors. He reached in before I could move and grabbed me, throwing me over his massive shoulder. Heading straight for the house, I pounded on his back as he walked into the house and up the stairs, "Let me go!"

Still nothing from him. Until he walked into a bedroom, "Here is the doctor." He said as he let me down on my feet. "I took one of the ambulances too, just in case you needed... I don't know something from it." He explained to the group of people around, then he looked at me,
"Sorry, ma'am for the rough treatment, but as you can see it is an emergency." He gestured towards the woman laying on her stomach on the bed in the room, then turned and left the room. Leaving me standing there looking at the injured woman; dark nearly black blood had stained the mattress under her. Four others were staring at me.

"What happened to her?" I asked, finally as my medical training set me into action.

"She was shot, with this." One of the onlookers said holding out a bullet in his hand. "It went through her and hit Grayson in the hip. I think it hit her liver." He gestured to a massive redheaded Lycan standing bare-chested over the woman lying there.

Looking around at all of them standing there, "I need to examine her, could I have some privacy please." I explained when no one moved fast enough, "OUT!" I yelled.

Three of them left as the largest looked down at the woman, then back to me, "I'm staying." He informed me.

I had a feeling that arguing with him would be senseless, so I nodded, "I need to get her clothes off." Looking around, "Do you have any scissors?"

My suspicions were confirmed when he extended a razor-sharp nail from his finger and sliced through the woman's clothes. I didn't explain why I was not afraid, or shocked, but he seemed to want to let me know. "There are reasons we could not take her to a human hospital." He stated. "You don't need to worry, no one here will harm you." Looking up at me explaining, then back to the woman on the bed.

Nodding, "I heard stories about all of you." That was all I would give him as a reason for not being afraid. Then I looked at the injury to the woman, "Your friend is probably right, this black blood looks like it hit her liver. But unless she is bleeding internally, there isn't a lot of it." Looking up at the massive man, "Is she your wife?"

I knew that was not the proper word, but saying mate, would give me away, I assumed he just thought I was a normal human when he just nodded, then asked, "What does she need?" His voice was laced with worry.

Sighing, "The one that brought me here, I need some things out of the ambulance."

"Noah," he called out, as his friend came in the tall one covering the female's naked body. "The doctor needs some things from the ambulance, go with her, and help bring up what she needs." He ordered.

Noah, nodded, "Of course. Follow me, please." Stepping back, he let me pass.

When we reached the ambulance parked outside of the house, he opened the back and helped me inside. Pulling open drawers, I gathered what I thought I would need, handing them to my capture. Then I could not believe my eyes, there was a portable sonogram machine, I only prayed it worked. I followed him through the house, where the other three that were in the room as well as a few more, I assumed, friends, gathered around with worried looks on their faces. I tried to smile, to reassure them, but it was fruitless, I didn't know what I was facing with her injury, and I may not be able to save her.

Once back up to the bedroom, I explained that I needed to start an IV. The huge man leaned down whispering to his mate when she moaned, "I am here mo chara, lay still the doctor is here." He whispered, surprisingly it calmed her.

Startled, I glanced up, "Mate?" I whispered, then quickly I looked back down at the task of inserting the needle into the woman's arm, "My grandmother was raised in Scotland, she taught me," a lie, I just hoped he didn't question me further about my knowledge of Gaelic. "There," I said putting the last of the tape to secure the port now in her arm.

My only reason for explaining each thing I did was I was nervous. The massive man finally said, "Doctor, I am old. But I know the names of your medical procedures." Thankfully he didn't seem upset, I would hate to see him when he was angry.

With a quick nod, I told him about finding the ultrasound in the ambulance, and that it may help me see what was going on inside of his mate. Calling out for his friend, he turned her over onto her back, then as I pressed the wand to her abdomen. It was causing her pain, and he barked at me with frustration.

Pulling the wand away, I stood up pointing to the monitor as his friend left the room, "There. It looks like the bullet passed through just grazing the side of her liver." I looked at him making sure he was understanding what I was telling him. Now came the good news, bad news, I stood up beside the bed, "Even if I attempted surgery, I can't repair her liver. That's the bad news." Sighing, "A blood transfusion might work, but it may not save her life. But I could not see large amounts of blood accumulating. That's the good news."

A woman and man were in the doorway, and a heated discussion ensued about giving this woman, a human woman their blood. They didn't seem to care, I was a stranger to them, and saving this woman's life was all that mattered. Finally, the massive man decided, to give her his blood, holding out his arm, "Do what you need to do," He ordered.

When I questioned him about their blood types not matching, he just calmly said, "Doctor, I am a Lycan. Victoria is human, we are fated, mates. Our blood will be compatible. As you heard, my blood has self-healing powers. Please do what you need to give her my blood, or I will have Jackson come in and do it for you."

Against my Hippocratic oath, I inserted the needle in his arm, and quickly the bag filled with his blood, sighing, and praying I had not just killed his mate, I hooked the bag up to the port I had placed in her arm earlier. I knew all about Lycan blood having healing powers, but no one had given a human this much Lycan blood ever. When humans were turned thousands of years ago, they were given Lycan blood in small amounts over a course of time. Whispering my fear, "I hope you are right, or I just may have killed her." Then the events of this afternoon were starting to weigh on my mind and body, I plopped down in a nearby chair and thought out loud. "They will come looking for that ambulance."

He stood to shake my hand, saying he would have his friend take me back to the hospital, then he said, "Thank you for coming. And, doctor, we all would appreciate it if you would not discuss what happened here. You can understand that we would be hunted down if humans knew of our existence here."

I understand more than you know, I kept that thought to myself, then I said, "I will come up with some excuse as to why we took the ambulance." I glanced over to the bed at his mate, and asked, "I am off for the next few days, I want to come back and stay with her to make sure she is going to be okay. With your permission of course."

He expressed his gratitude, then called for his friend, "Take the doctor and the ambulance back. And let the guards at the gate know that she will be returning."

As I left the room, I watched as he sat down in a chair beside the bed, his eyes transfixed on his mate. *Now that is true devotion.* I thought. When I got back to the hospital, there had been an eight-car accident out on the highway, and I ended up not having to answer a lot of questions about the missing ambulance. I helped and stayed longer than my shift until everything calmed down. Then I found out the name of the man they had brought in and checked up on him before I left to go home.

The next morning, I drove back out to the compound, nervous that I would be rejected, but it wasn't so. I was greeted cordially and with thanks for wanting to help his human mate. So, I spent the next several days keeping watch over Victoria, she remained unconscious, and Grayson her mate, had never left her side.

Finally, she woke up, and when I examined her wounds, there was barely a mark to be seen, I knew the feeling, though they didn't know it I had Lycan blood flowing through my veins, and scars were never a part of my life.

Chapter 5

Murdoc

Only three days after Grayson's incident, when Lucas called again. As I laid my phone back down on my desk, I just hung up. Victoria, a human, and my brother's mate had been shot by the same human that shot him. Her injury was life-threatening, and Grayson, going against one of our most sacred laws, gave her a large amount of his blood. She was still unconscious but alive. Not only that, but they had exposed themselves to a human doctor. Pacing back and forth, I needed to make calls to the High Council and the other Princes. Against our laws or not, I will not have my brother persecuted for this.

Hours I spent on the phone, with council members and the other princes. Thankfully they agreed it was a dire situation, and any of us would do the same if one of our mates was about to die without our healing blood. I also spent time catching up with my lifelong friends, when we each took over our titles, we were spread out across the globe.

A knock came on my study door, "Enter," I called out.

MacDonald walked in, "Is it true?" Growling, sometimes I hated how gossip moved through a clan.

Sitting on the corner of my desk, I crossed my arms over my chest, "What?"

Getting right to the point, "Did Grayson give a human his blood?" He crossed his arms over his chest, disgust written all over his face. "A HUMAN?" he growled.

He was nearing my breaking point with his hatred of humans. "You mean my brother, Grayson Ewan Sinclair his Grace, Duke of Arcadia?" I stood and growled the question, "Yes, he saved his mate's life. Is there a problem?"

Not knowing when to back down, "She is a human, and it is against our laws. What if she turns into one of us?" Seething now.

"I am well aware of our laws." Still growling at his disrespectful tone toward me, I didn't even touch the subject that Grayson could have turned her into a Lycan with the amount of blood he gave her.

"Will they be put to death?" he asked, almost excited at the prospect.

"No," I answered quietly, but he didn't realize the danger he was in.

Taken back by my answer, "You mean because you used your title and influence to intervene and got your brother out of this mess?"

I had reached my breaking point, I stood and stepped closer to my commander, we were about the same age, but I was still larger and stronger. My fangs came out as I grew with each step, "You will leave my sight this instant before I remove your head," my beast growled.

Taking the smart choice, MacDonald lowered his head and backed out of my office, the hatred was still plastered all over his face. As the door closed, I calmed down, lowering my head, this had gone on for far too long.

Picking my phone back up to make another call, but before I could, my phone rang. It was my sister. "Murdoc, I need your help," she said as a greeting.

Sighing, my sister rarely called me for help, she was mated to a respected leader of a Lycan Clan, strong in his own right. "What's going on, Bea?"

"Amira," she sighed. "And her companion."

"Isabelle MacDonald," offering my niece's companion's name. The daughter of my commander.

"Yes," sighing again, "Isabelle has Amira showing such hatred toward other beings, I just can't deal with it any longer." Then I heard her voice hitch, "With the babe coming, I need a break."

Realizing I had almost forgotten that my sister was expecting again, "How about I send the jet?" I offered.

Relief was evident in her voice, "Thank you, Murdoc."

"Bea?" I was not sure that this was the best time to tell her, so I hedged. "Have you heard from Grayson?"

"We know," she said. "I hope she survives; Grayson deserves to be happy." Pausing, "Murdoc, Amira knows too, and please see what you can do."

Disconnecting the call, I called in my second in command and ordered the jet with a guard detail to go and pick up my niece and her companion.

Then I made the call I had intended to make, "We just talked," Liam Cain said on the other end.

"I know, I need some advice." I sighed.

"What's going on?" he asked. I spent the next hour explaining the prejudices in my clan, from a few of the elders to my first in command, and now my niece is coming for an extended stay.

Liam listened to the issue and huffed when I finished. "Prejudice is a problem with every being. But you are a prince and the head of your clan, meet with the elders. Let them know you will not tolerate these prejudices any longer."

Stopping for a moment. "Murdoc, it probably will not work, prejudice is nearly impossible to get out of anyone. And you may have to force out those who will not follow you." He spoke again. "And if you need my help, just call."

I had a feeling that is what it was going to come down to, forcing out members of my clan was not something I wanted to do, but matters had gotten out of hand.

Chapter 6

Melissa

After spending three days tending to Victoria, I left a few hours after she woke up. Then going back only a handful of times to check on her. I had heard the argument about giving her Lycan blood, and I knew it was forbidden. I also knew that many of his powers probably transferred to her, if not even turning her into a Lycan. Victoria was nice, as was Samantha, the other female in the compound. I gave both Grayson and Lucas my card in case they had another need for medical attention.

But I went back to my daily life, with no word from them. Esmee came to me several times over the weeks that followed, always telling me that 'he was coming'. I knew she meant my mate. That made me nervous at the prospect of meeting him. This wasn't like dating, which I had not done a lot of. Becoming a doctor took up a lot of time, and since I chose to be a surgeon as well, let's just say my social life was nonexistent. I didn't even have any social media accounts, there wasn't any need, my parents died years ago, and I had no siblings. Which was unusual for Lycans, as we are known for large families.

So, I just kept my head down and waited for a call to come from one of them. I didn't feel right just barging onto their compound. They would ask questions, and I tried to avoid questions as much as possible. Over my short life, I learned the appropriate answers that satisfied most humans about my life. Why were my eyes bluer at times over others? 'Oh, it was probably the light.' You cut healed, and you don't have a scar or a mark? 'Just good genes I guess.' And the questions would go on and on.

These Lycans would ask different questions, ones I was not sure I had the answers to that would appease them. That made me stay away and wait for a call if it came at all. And it did come some weeks later.

Lucas was the one that called me, "Dr. Herbert, I am sorry to ask. But we have another situation here. Could you come out to the compound?"

Smiling on the other end, "I can leave in a few minutes." Then I asked some quick questions to make sure I brought with me what necessary medical supplies I needed. After I arrived, I tended to the man that had caused so much trouble for my new friends. His throat was severely bruised and swollen and other than some pain medication and recommending ice, there was not much I could do.

Knocking on Lucas' door, he opened it, and I came in. Smiling, he looked like his grandfather, whom he didn't know I knew about. So, I kept that information to myself. But his look became intense, "Your eyes changed color." He said matter-of-factly. Then tilting his head to the side, thinking I could not hear him, he whispered, *"bana-bhuidseach,"* witch in Gaelic.

Lowering my head, I blinked a couple of times to get my eyes to return to their normal shade of blue, then looked up at him, "Not entirely a witch," I offered as an explanation.

Pointing to his office on the right, "Sit," it was an order.

Then he went around to his desk and sat down, looking straight at me. "Before I begin, I would appreciate this conversation not leaving this room," I said.

Just like his grandfather, his right eyebrow shot up at least an inch. "That depends on what you have to tell me."

Smiling, "I am sure your grandmother told you about her sister Esmee." It wasn't a question.

Nodding he didn't say anything, "I am her..." I stopped for a moment, "descendant," I finally said. I didn't look away from him, "After she left the compound in Northern Scotland, she traveled to Germany where she met her mate. Martio."

He was remembering the stories, "He was the Lycan leader that helped your grandfathers when Grayson's father was born."

Finally breaking his silence, "You have Lycan and Witch blood." I nodded.

'Tell him the rest.' Esmee encouraged.

Taking a deep breath, "Esmee cast a spell on me before she died. Binding both my witch and Lycan powers until I meet my fated mate."

"How old are you?" He asked.

"Twenty-eight." I smiled.

"Esmee died..." He stopped trying to remember the year.

"In 1525. While she was giving birth to a daughter," I said. The look he was giving me was disbelieving, "Esmee like her sister, Noémie, your grandmother could both see into the future. She foretold many threats to my life and decided if I was perceived to be a human, she could keep me safe. So, she cast a spell to bind my powers, giving her life and the life of her unborn daughter so I may live."

A small smile formed, "So you and I are related?"

Chuckling, "After all that, you want to know if we are related?" Sighing, "Yes, I suppose we are. Lucas, please, I would prefer that this conversation stays between us."

"She is your cousin, Lucas you have to protect her." Samantha quietly said from the doorway. I jumped at the sound of her voice.

Lucas grinned, "Samantha is right, we are related. We can protect you here."

Shaking my head, "No, I can't just disappear from my life. I am a doctor, and have worked long and hard to get where I am."

Samantha walked in, before she could sit Lucas stood and helped her into the chair beside me. "Where are your parents?" She asked as soon as she was seated.

"Dead." I lowered my head, "About eleven years ago. I was away in college when it happened," I uttered the last.

"Do you not have any other family?" Lucas asked.

"No, I am an only child. I know that is somewhat unusual for a Lycans." I shrugged my shoulders.

Samantha reached over covering my hand with hers, "Not so unusual, I am an only child as well." She looked up at Lucas, "Well?"

Lucas shook his head, "Well, what? I can't make her stay here." He put up his hand at his mate's huff. "But we can provide you with security." He said to me.

I started to shake my head before he finished his sentence, "There is no need, for now, I am a human. And no one knows of my bloodline other than you two. As I said, I would prefer to keep it that way." I stood, and reached over to Samantha, shaking her hand, "Warm baths will help." I offered advice. Then turned to face Lucas, "You have my number if you need me, cousin."

Lucas looked at his wife, "You stay there." Then he walked me to my car. "If you need anything, call me, Melissa."

Laughing as I reached for the door handle. "You found out fifteen minutes ago we are related, and now you are acting like my protector."

Lucas didn't seem to like my response, he lowered his face to mine as his eyes glowed red, growling deep and menacing. "Okay, I'll call," I conceded.

Before I could shut the door to my car, "Drive safe." Then he shut the door. I could see him in my rearview mirror standing with his legs apart and arms crossed over his chest. From what Esmee has told me and shown me, he is the image of his grandfather, and just as menacing.

Arriving home, I slept hard and dreamless. Esmee had left me alone for the night. I felt refreshed the next morning and decided to go for a run, and that is when I saw them, the two of them, Lucas, had not heeded my wishes and placed a security detail on me. Getting home I texted him, "You can call off your men. They are going to dredge up more questions than I need."

He replied with one word, "Denied."

That evening, he called, "Come to dinner on Friday."

Laughing, "I can't."

"Melissa." I could hear the warning tone in his voice.

"I am on duty this weekend. Doctor. Remember?" I laughed.

He sighed on the other end, "When are you off duty then?"

"Monday and Tuesday." I offered.

"Monday then." He said, "Eight, we will eat after the babes are asleep." His voice deepened, "Don't be late."

Looking up I could see a nurse waiving me down, "I won't. I have to go, Lucas." And I hung up on him and ran to the next emergency.

Chapter 7

Murdoc

These last weeks have been one trail on my nerves after another. Amira, more than old enough to be mated, was a handful. I spoke daily to Bea and assured her that I was trying my best to get Amira to see that humans were not all bad, nor were any other beings in our world that should be hated.

Grayson had called, telling me that Victoria had turned into a Lycan. Eryn had come and visited with her, and she was now dealing with a huge change in her life. Before hanging up he invited me to come and officiate his mating ceremony to Victoria. The thought crossed my mind to take Amira with me, but she refused to be anywhere near his mate.

"Your uncle would be happy to see you, Amira," I said crossing my arms over my chest.

"I don't want to go," she honestly pouted.

"You are not a pup, stop pouting," I growled.

"I want to go home." She honestly pouted again.

"Bea, I mean your mother just birthed. She does not need you being difficult right now," then lowering my head coming nose to nose with her, "Stop pouting like a pup," I growled.

She raised her chin in defiance when I pulled away, "Are you going to make me go?"

Sighing, "No, I don't want you ruining Grayson's ceremony. And I could use a few days away from you as well." I didn't hide my exasperation and irritation. Pointing to the door, "You may go."

Pivoting around on her feet, she huffed, but before she could make it to the doorway of my study, "Amira, did you forget something?"

Glaring at me over her shoulder, she curtsied, "Your Highness." It was a sneer, and she was acting like a brat. I pitied the one that would end up being her mate. I hope he has a strong will, he will need it with her. I left my study and headed up to my room, one of the servants had laid out some of my clothes so that I could pack. Unlike some older Lycans, I did away with the tradition of having a valet, when my last one passed.

As I finished my packing to leave, MacDonald came to see me, "I am ready to go, your highness."

"You're not coming with me," I said, not explaining.

"I am your first in command," He argued.

"You're not coming with me," I stated again. "You will stay here and protect Amira. I have others to come and watch my back. Besides I am going to a compound that is full of Knights of Arcadia, I will be safe."

Just then I saw it, a flash of something in his eyes. "As you wish, your highness."

As I walked past him, "Amira is my niece, and I am trusting you as my first in command to keep her safe and out of trouble while I am gone." I don't know why I was saying this, it was all a lie, I was not even sure how long MacDonald was going to remain my first in command. I had not spoken to anyone other than Liam, but I felt some changes needed to be made within my clan. But it seemed to appease him. Good.

Arriving the night before the ceremony, I didn't get to see much of Grayson or Victoria before it was time to officiate the ceremony. Lucas invited me to stay with him and Samantha, but with the babes, I stayed with Noah instead. Lucas laughed, slapping me on the back, "As you wish, but soon you will have a castle full of squalling young." Then he told me that there would be two humans in attendance, a doctor that helped save Victoria's life, and her father.

The hour of the ceremony had come, and my attention as I walked up to the edge of the mating circle was on Victoria, she was a pretty thing, and I could smell she was nervous. I didn't think she was afraid of me, surely not, if she was standing here waiting to be officially mated to my brother.

As Lucas and the other members of the Knights filed through the trees before Grayson, a scent filled my nostrils, and I turned just my eyes to the human female standing on the edge of the circle to my right. My beast stirred, *"Mine,"* his growl was low so low I was sure that only I heard him.

Pulling my attention back to the ceremony, I was able to get through it without grabbing the female and throwing her over my shoulder, and running to the forest.

During the celebration I stood back and watched, her eyes were the purest of blues, and her hair was long a reddish-brown as the color of the wild cherry trees near my home. She was tall for a female, but I could tell she was not a child, maybe in her mid-twenties. She was in a dress that was not overly exposing herself. Good, she was mine, and I didn't want any-one else looking at her. She has a woman's body, firm breasts, round hips, and an ass I could not wait to grasp as I drove into her while mating. But there was something about her that kept me here standing across the room watching her. Just once I thought I saw her look my way, and in a flash, her eyes changed to the purest blue. I had seen this only once in my life, Lucas' grandmother. I barely remember her as a pup, but I knew she was a witch.

True witches had not been around for centuries, many in Europe were burned alive. When I was just taking over as Prince, there had been rumors that we now know to be true that even here in the United States women and even men accused of witchcraft were prosecuted and put to death just if it was thought that they were witches. If a full-blooded witch was alive today, they hid their powers and hid away from hu-mans. Some claimed to be witches, but they were just humans playing pretend. This human, my mate could not be a witch. Maybe it was just the light here in Lucas' house that made me think her eyes changed color. Realizing someone had made a toast to the happy couple. Lifting my glass of champagne to my mouth, not even knowing what I was toasting to. When the bubbles reached my lips, I pretended to take a drink, I hated champagne. Glancing over the rim of my glass I saw that my mate did the same, as she lowered her glass, with a smile plastered on her face, she crinkled up her nose. Then Grayson and Victoria left the celebration, I knew that they would be headed to the woods.

Feeling eyes on me, I looked around. There with his arm around Samantha, Lucas was watching me, an eyebrow raised in question at my reactions to this human. I was not about to explain myself to him. Nodding my head and raising my glass in salute, then I laid it down on a side table and slipped out through the French doors. I needed some air, and time to think, I would not dare go out to the woods and risk intruding on the newly mated couple. So, I just headed to Noah's and sat out on the back porch.

When Lucas walked my mate out to her car and spoke to her before she left, I heard them. Standing I moved around between the houses and watched until Lucas walked back into his home. Removing my shirt, I let my beast come out, I was stronger and faster in my beast form, I ran after her keeping to the side of the road, and I followed her home.

Standing outside of her apartment building, I watched the lights turn on and her form walk through the rooms. Pulling her hair down, I could see that it nearly fell to her waist, I wanted to run my fingers through it, I am sure it would feel like mink. A movement caught my attention, and I turned my head. There were two of them standing off to the side watching her building, neither was looking up at her second-floor window. I knew them, they were some of the Orders trainees under Lucas' command.

Stepping out of the shadows I let them see me then moved toward them. One growled at me, the other recognizing me bowed his head, "Your Highness" as he nudged the other still showing me his fangs.

Catching on to who I was, he too bowed his head, "My apologies, your highness."

Nodding, I crossed my arms and braced my legs, "Why are you guarding the doctor?" I was not about to tell them she was my mate.

Looking at each other then back to me, "We were ordered to." the one told me.

"I assumed you were ordered to, but why were you ordered to protect her?" trying to clarify my question.

"We don't know. Commander Cain just ordered us to watch out for her." The second answered.

Frustrated, I was not ready to announce the doctor was my mate, I had to think. She is human and bringing her home will cause problems in my clan. I needed to clear up those problems before I claimed her. The two guards were just staring at me these last few minutes as I tried to sort all this out in my head.

"If I command you, will you follow my order?" It was a stretch, but I had to try.

Both snapped up, "Yes sir." I nearly rolled my eyes, these two were young, I was at least a good two hundred years older than they are.

"I do not wish for anyone to know I was here. You are ordered not to tell any of the other trainees or your commanders. Especially Commander Cain. Understood?" I spoke.

Both dropped open their mouths, "We... Of course, your highness." Both agreed. I had a feeling that neither would keep their word, I was not their commander. Being a prince had some advantages, but these two reported to Lucas. I sighed and turned to leave, but not before glancing once more up at her apartment windows. Her shadow moved around as she did, the lights turned off one by one, and she was going to bed. As I walked back to the compound, I wondered if she had noticed me watching her. Or if she knew about the guards outside of her apartment.

Chapter 8

Melissa

A Lycan mating ceremony was exciting. My mother had told me about hers, the beauty and splendor of being offi-cially claimed by my father. She described the circle, and the officiant looking stern the whole time. This one was different, Grayson was descended from royalty, and there was only one royal family in the Lycan world, the descendants of Lycaon himself. My mate was going to be here tonight, Esmee told me. So, I wanted to look my best. I dressed in the only special dress I had, a deep blue chiffon that was high-waisted and flowed out at the skirt. I did my hair up in a French knot on the back of my head, letting loose wisps fall around my face. Never one for a lot of makeup, I tried to stay as natural as possible. I was tall, and I knew we would be out in the forest, so I wore a pair of black slipper flats. They were the only dress shoes I owned, normally the only things that were on my feet were the sneak-ers I wore at work or my running shoes.

When I arrived, I was led out to the mating circle and shown where I was to stand at the edge of the circle. I looked up flowers that had been weaved in and out through the branches of the trees above our heads. It was beautiful. As the full moon was nearly at its pinnacle is when I got my first glance at him. Murdoc walked up and stood just ten feet from me. His eyes were focused on Victoria. Then just for a second, I felt his eyes on me, I could have sworn I heard his beast. It was so low I was not sure.

Something inside of me stirred, *"He is your mate, your beast is awakening,"* Esmee explained. Resisting the urge to rub my chest, I looked my fill at him, dressed in black trousers like the others, he had on a crisp white shirt, it was tight against his chest, and I could only imagine what he looked like without it. A tartan sash of blue and white, the colors of his clan draped across his shoulder, and over his heart were two pendants the first of the royal crest, made of diamonds and rubies, the second of the crest of his clan, made with diamonds and sapphires. Grayson and each of the others wore a breastplate that had the same royal crest engraved on it. As I listened to him talk. His voice was a baritone, deep with his Scottish accent it felt like he was speaking to my heart.

As soon as the ceremony was over everyone moved to Lucas and Samantha's home for a feast. I mingled around, speaking with Victoria's father, and met Fergus Samantha's father. I felt his eyes on me each time I moved or spoke to someone. Once when I thought for certain he was not watching I looked at him. His penetrating gaze lifted to mine; I realized my eyes changed when he blinked at me. Quickly I lowered my eyes until they came back to their normal color.

He was my mate, I felt it the second I laid eyes on him at the mating circle, fated to be together, but something was holding me back from going up to him. Another toast was being made to the happy couple, and I lifted my glass of champagne to my lips, but I have never been a drinker. So, I pretended to sip, then finally I laid my glass down and walked over to Lucas and Samantha. Lucas' eyes on me were penetrating, "What's happened?" He asked.

"Nothing," was all the answer he was going to get from me. I heard a low growl, as his eyes looked up at Murdoc.

Smiling and being as polite as possible, "I have an early shift tomorrow, I need to get home. Thank you for inviting me."

Samantha looked up at Lucas, nudging him. "Lucas, walk Melissa out to her car."

Lucas was lost in thought, "Hmm, What?"

Samantha shook her head, "Melissa is leaving, walk her out, please."

Lucas motioned to the front door and opened it for me. When we got to my car, "You would tell me if something was wrong?" He phrased it as a question, but I felt the demand in the tone of his voice.

"Probably not," I smiled, "Unless, of course, it was life-threatening." I corrected when his eyes flashed. Changing the subject, "Are you going to call off my security?"

"Probably not," he grinned repeating to me. "You are my cousin and have no one to protect you until you get your powers. Until that time, you are my responsibility."

Shaking my head, "Esmee was wrong, you are a worse bully than your grandfather," I laughed at the outraged look on his face at my statement, sliding into the driver's seat. Looking up at him, "Lucas, I am an adult and have not been anyone's responsibility since my parents died." Not wanting to argue with him, which I knew was fruitless, I pulled my door closed than started my car, and pulled out to the main road.

There was an eerie feeling of someone following me, as I drove. With each glance in my rearview mirror, I could not see anything or anyone following me. Finally pulling into my parking spot at my apartment, I looked around as I got out, then hurried up the stairs to unlock my door. Once inside I quickly relocked the door and leaned against it for a moment, this was all Lucas' fault, he had my nerves on edge. Pulling my phone from my bag, I thought of calling Lucas but decided against it. Esmee would have warned me of any danger. That was one thing Lucas didn't know about my guardian witch grandmother that kept watch over me.

Moving about my apartment I flipped on every light. I still had that feeling that someone was watching me, so I peeked out the window. I saw the two Lycans that Lucas had assigned to watch me. Maybe it was them I sensed. Now I felt like a fool, between Lucas' over-protectiveness and the security watching my every move. Now I had to turn off every light before I could go to bed. Once I thought about it, I slept in many doctor lounges that were lit up like the Las Vegas strip with no problem, but when I was home, I liked it dark.

Sleep evaded me, Murdoc's eyes watching me at the festivities, probably what unnerved me this evening. I was sure I heard his beast, but he made no move toward me. Maybe he has not realized I am to be his mate. That was a disturbing thought. Another was he is one of the Princes of Arcadia, high-ranking in the Lycan world, did he avoid me because he didn't want me as a mate? I flopped over onto my stomach, raising my head just for a moment to look at the clock on my side table, four AM. I had to be at the hospital at eight, well I have worked on less sleep. I closed my eyes and hummed.

Chapter 9

Murdoc

After my little talk with the security watching Melissa, I walked back to the compound, thankfully when I arrived everything was quiet, and I snuck back into Noah's house. Her scent still drifted into my nose, a sensual mixture of jasmine and vanilla. When I closed my eyes, I could see her standing there at the side of the mating circle, dressed in blue. The color matched her eyes, not a provocative dress, but my hands still itched to shred it off her, to caress the skin underneath.

How was I going to find out the reason that Lucas is protecting her? Could she be a part of one of their missions? That was highly unlikely. Then I remembered seeing her eyes change, could she be a witch? Was she in hiding, and Lucas was protecting her? I needed answers before I claimed her. But I was only going to be here for a few days, I needed to work fast. Then when I got home, I needed to clean out the prejudice in my clan before I brought my mate there. I would not put her in danger.

As soon as the sun rose, I was back up and out of bed. I had heard her say she had an early morning shift at the hospital, and I intended to go and see her again. But first, I needed to get my security detail occupied so I could be alone. They were up and waiting for me as I walked out of Noah's house. "You are going to train with the others today," I announced, leaving no room for arguments.

They all nodded, not suspecting that I intended on leaving the compound's safety. We walked to the training fields and stood watching for a few minutes, looking around. "Well, go!" I ordered. Smiling at the prospect of bashing some young Lycan heads, they ran off stripping to the waist as they went. I turned and nearly ran into Lucas standing behind me. "Lucas," I greeted him.

Lucas bowed his head, "Your Highness," and then he looked me straight in the eye. "A word please?" And motioned for me to follow him. We moved away from shouting and grunting going on as the training continued. "You followed Melissa last night. Why?"

Not answering his question, "Why are you protecting her?" I countered.

Lucas smiled, "Is she your mate?"

All I could do was close my eyes, "Yes. But I don't want it to be known yet. Why are you protecting her, is it due to one of your missions?"

Lucas crossed his arms, "No, it is a family matter."

"As far as I know you only had one sister that perished as a pup," I stated, "Who is she to you?"

Lucas was getting agitated; he didn't like being questioned any more than I did. "That is true, my sister Margot died at three. And Melissa has asked that I keep her identity secret, which I intend on doing." I was about to say something when he asked a question, "Do the problems in your clan have anything to do with your not claiming her?"

It was my turn to chuckle, "Your brother has a big mouth." I shook my head, "Some, yes. I need to clean house so to speak before I would bring her home."

Lucas nodded, "I will not let her go if she is in danger there."

It was my turn to cross my arms, "Nor would I put her in danger." There was loud cheering that came from the field and we both turned at the sound.

"I was going to see her today at the hospital. Where is it?" It was a demand, I only hoped he answered, there could be any number of hospitals.

Chuckling, "She won't like you intruding on her work." Before I could bark at him, "Mercy Hospital off Main. Take one of Grayson's bikes, he is a little preoccupied today."

I turned to head to the barn, "She's headstrong, Murdoc. I would not try the whole 'I'm a Prince and you will obey me' thing with her."

I thought that statement was funny until she spotted me standing back in the human emergency room watching her. Like a bull that saw red, she came charging at me, glaring. When she reached me, "What are you doing here?" tapping her foot but not waiting for me to respond, "Are you sick, hurt, injured?"

Only grinning at her absurd question, she reached out and grabbed my hand, "Come with me." It was a demand, and I let her have her way.

Walking into a room with cots and lockers lining the walls, "Murdoc, tell Lucas I do not want any security. This is too much, I am working."

Confused, "Lucas didn't send me. Your security is outside."

She closed her eyes, and lowered her head, "Then why are you here?"

A knock came on the door, and a human woman looked in, "Doctor Herbert there is an accident coming in, at least three."

Melissa turned and nodded toward the nurse, "I will be right there," she said to the other woman, when she turned back to me, "I have lives to save, Murdoc. Please leave."

"I have not given you permission to use my name," I was doing just what Lucas told me not to.

Exasperated, "Isn't your name, Murdoc?" I nodded, and she continued, "And I didn't give you permission to invade my workplace." Sirens were getting closer. She turned to leave, "Go back to the compound Murdoc." She called over her shoulder and then as the sirens stopped outside the building, she sprinted out the door. I followed her, doing the exact opposite of what she asked, I leaned up against the same empty spot on the wall and watched.

As a human was being brought in on a gurney, someone called out, "He's crashing." Without hesitation Melissa jumped up straddling the man and started to pump his chest, to get his heart beating again. Calling out orders for nurses and orderlies to carry out, they all jumped and did her bidding. I was amazed and proud of her.

She was running from room to room attending to the humans, and I understood their lives depended on her. For at least three hours this went on, and she didn't stop for a second. Attending to those humans that were hurt, and holding hands as spoke softly to their families as they arrived.

Finally, when everything calmed down, I watched as she walked up to me again, "Murdoc, I am not a sideshow."

"Why is Lucas protecting you?" I asked.

"Follow me your royal pain in the ass." She walked away, as she passed one of the nurses, "I'll be in the cafeteria."

The nurse nodded and grinned at me as I followed Melissa seeing the nurse's reaction she grumbled, "That is exactly why I don't want you here. Questions."

Finally, in the cafeteria, she grabbed a couple of bottles one of each juice and water, walking over to a register, I pulled out my wallet and tried to hand the woman standing at the register my credit card.

Melissa placed her hand on mine to stop me, "Thank you, Megan." She said and signed a receipt. Walking over she sat at a table, and closing her eyes she rubbed the back of her neck before she looked at me. There again, her eyes changed.

She didn't try to hide it from me this time, "You're a witch." It was a statement. "Is that why Lucas is protecting you?" I wanted and needed answers. "He said it was a family matter."

She chuckled, "Yes and no. To your first statement." Smiling at me. I guess the look on my face was funny. She knew I was not used to or liked getting vague answers, "I didn't ask or want Lucas' protection. And a very distant family matter." She finished with her vague answers.

Crossing my arms over my chest, I was about to bark at her until I realized where we were. Humans were mingling about. "I am not amused, Melissa." Growling low.

She placed her hands on the table and leaned forward, "In this building, you will address me as Dr. Herbert," her voice was stern and unwavering, "I have worked my ass off to get where I am, and no one, including a Prince, is going to take that from me." She looked around and whispered the last part.

Leaning back, she reached for a bottle of water, and handed it to me, before grabbing the orange juice. She opened it and drank it down. Looking at her watch, "I need to get back to the ER, nice talking to you." She stood and walked out. I sat there and looked at the now vacant doorway. Smiling, Lucas was right, she is stubborn.

When I got back to the emergency room, I looked around and found her talking to a nurse, then signed a chart. She looked up at me and glared. I raised my hands in surrender and left out the doors. I leaned against Grayson's bike in the parking lot for hours until she finally came out, then I followed her home.

Walking up to her, I didn't say a thing, "Murdoc, I am tired. I just worked twelve hours. All I want to do is take a long hot bath and go to bed. Please leave." She sounded exhausted, so I walked her to her door and waited for her to unlock the door.

Holding out my hand, "Give me your phone." She was exhausted and didn't argue, just reached into her bag, pulled out her phone, and handed it to me. I punched in my number and felt the vibrations as it rang in my pocket. "Are you working tomorrow?" She shook her head no, "I'll call you tomorrow."

She nodded, then I placed two fingers under her chin, her eyes met mine, as I lowered my head and kissed her lightly. "We need to talk; before I leave in a couple of days."

Confused and taken back, "You're leaving?"

"Yes, I need to get back home," I answered unsure of her confusion. But she looked crushed at the news that I was leaving.

Turning and going inside, "Goodbye, Murdoc." She whispered and closed the door, and I heard the lock click in place. Not that it would stop me if I wanted to get to her, I would just tear the door apart. When I got back to the parking lot and kickstarted Grayson's bike, I saw the two assigned to guard her in place for the night. Pulling out I drove back to the compound; the look on her face when I told her I was leaving stayed on my mind on the drive back and as I lay here trying to sleep, I cannot get out of my head.

Chapter 10

Melissa

After I locked the door, I leaned against it until I heard his footsteps retreating down the stairs. He is leaving, that is what he said, in a couple of days. What did this mean? He didn't want me as his mate. But why then did he kiss me? A tear slipped down my cheek, I have not shed a tear since my parents died. Angrily I wiped it away, who cares? I am fine just as I am. I never asked to be some powerful Lycan witch. Pushing away from the door I looked out the living room window, watching as the motorcycle lights turned and disappeared down the road. Glancing to the right, where my two guards stood in the shadows. I am going to have to talk to Lucas about this, I am done being followed around.

The long hot bath didn't help my mood but did help my sore muscles. Emotionally and physically exhausted, I fell asleep nearly as fast as my head hit my pillow. When I woke up, I was just as weary as I was when I went to bed. The visions I had were terrifying, not dreams, visions. Esmee and Noémie both were able to see into the future, if that is what I was seeing, I wanted no part of it. Dark caves, the terrifying feeling of impending death, I even saw Murdoc changed to a wall, straining to get loose.

Contemplating going back to bed, I jumped at the sound of my phone ringing. It was an unknown number, so I didn't answer it. Probably just some telemarketer. Looking out the window, they were still there, my protectors. This whole situation was giving me a headache, I turned and headed back to my room, maybe if I get a couple more hours of sleep, I will feel better, my phone rang again. Same unknown number, answering, "What!" I yelled, "I don't need any help with my student loans. I didn't have any! Stop calling me." I was agitated and tired.

"Melissa?" It was Murdoc. I was about to disconnect when I heard his voice.

Sighing, "Yes. What can I do for you Murdoc?"

"You sound tired, didn't you sleep well last night?" There was concern in his voice.

I wanted to reach through the phone and strangle him, "No, I didn't sleep well. I was going back to bed when someone kept calling me."

Chuckling, "Sorry. Why didn't you sleep well?"

I closed my eyes and counted to ten, "Questions. Have I mentioned I hate being asked questions?"

Chuckling at my response, "Yes, I heard you say something about that. Just one more and I will let you go back to bed." He didn't seem too apologetic about keeping me up.

"Go ahead. Ask."

"Will you please come out to the compound so we can talk?" I smiled, and he said 'please'.

But I was still a little unnerved about him leaving in a few days. "What is there to talk about, you are leaving?"

There was a growl on the other end, "Melissa, don't make me come there and throw you over my shoulder."

Gasping, "You'd do it too. Wouldn't you?"

There was a sinister tone, "After I ripped your door to shreds to get to you."

Grumbling, "Fine. I will text you when I am headed that way. I will see you later, Murdoc."

"Melissa, we need to get something settled now. I will address you as Doctor Herbert if I am ever at the hospital again. But in front of the others here at the compound, I need you to address me as 'Your Highness' or 'Prince' deal?"

Sarcastically, "Yes, Your Highness." Before he could say something more I hung up and turned off my phone then went back to bed. It was childish, but I grinned when I imagined the look that was probably on his face right now.

Chapter 11

'Headstrong' is what Lucas called her, stubborn, obstinate, contrary, and completely unruly. All those adjectives ran through my head as I looked at my phone, she just hung up on me. Shaking my head, I walked out of Noah's house, my security was waiting for me. An unusual smile was on my face, she would need all those qualities to be my mate and deal with a clan.

"Your Highness," my guard looked at me funny. "Is everything all right?"

That took the grin off my face, "Fine," nodding as I headed toward Lucas'. "Carry on with what you were doing yesterday or make yourselves useful around here."

"You are not planning on leaving the compound again?" he asked.

I turned, my eyes narrowing, and they flashed red, "Are you questioning me?"

Lowering his head, "No, Your Highness."

"I didn't think so, now leave me," I called over my shoulder.

Before I could knock, Lucas opened the door. Putting a finger to his lips, he held a sleeping babe to his shoulder, bowing his head, he then motioned for me to his study. Then he walked to the back of the house, coming back empty-handed, "Aileen has been giving us fits not sleeping at night." He explained. "I think I will have Melissa look at her."

"Your daughter is a Lycan," I said out loud.

"She is, but still a babe. Melissa may have an idea how to get her to sleep at night." He smiled and asked, "How was your visit to the hospital?"

Leaning back in the chair, "You were right, she didn't take me being there well. I think you are in for an earful when she comes. Melissa thought you sent me." Laughing, "I told her you didn't, but I am not sure she is happy with the security."

Lucas leaned back, "Too bad. She can complain all she wants unless she comes to stay here at the compound, she will have security."

"Will you tell me why you are you are protecting her?" I had hoped that we had gotten past his resistance to tell me.

"I am sorry, Murdoc. Melissa should be the one to explain."

Standing, "I will make her tell me then. I need answers before I go home," I grumbled.

Lucas grinned, "You just said she was not happy with you coming to the hospital. Do you think you can force her to tell you?"

Shaking my head, "She is like no other female I have come across." Talking to Lucas was getting me nowhere. Now I knew why he was so good at commanding the Knights, he would never break a confidence.

As I left Lucas' I spotted Grayson as he came out of his house, "Don't you have a mate to tend to?" I called out to my brother.

Meeting me halfway in the courtyard, "Victoria is out at the lake meditating or sleeping. I did wear her out." He laughed.

"Meditating?" I wondered.

He started to walk to the training fields, "It is helping her with controlling her beast."

Nodding that I understood, "How is she with all that?"

Grayson shrugged, "Her beast is like a pup, and will emerge without warning if she is emotional. But she is coping as best she can."

Thinking I could get some information from my brother, "What do you know about Dr. Herbert?"

Grayson was taller than me, only by an inch or two but I saw the sideways look he gave me, "Why?" He grinned.

Sighing, "She is my mate, but there are difficulties, with her and at home." Grayson didn't respond to my statement, and I needed to talk to someone other than Liam, and Lucas was not helping. "I have a clan that is full of prejudice. And I fear bringing Melissa there as my mate."

Grayson nodded, "MacDonald," it was a statement.

Shocked, I looked over to my brother, "What do you know?"

With a shrug, "Only that he has hated humans for as long as I have known him. He used to hide his feelings, but I take it he is not hiding his hatred any longer?"

"No, he had been quite verbal about it. And his ideas are trickling down into impressionable minds."

"Who's?" he growled.

"Clan members, his daughter, and now Amira," I listed off those I knew. "Amira is at my home for an extended visit; Bea needed some rest from her before the babe was born."

Grayson nodded again, "Is that why you didn't bring her to the mating ceremony?"

He didn't miss much, "Yes, and I needed a break from her too. But I didn't want her ruining your and Victoria's day." Getting back to the topic at hand, "I am planning on cleaning out those who will not follow me when I get home."

Grayson stopped walking, "It is probably for the best, but first I would talk to the high council. You don't want any trouble with them. There have not been any wars between clans within the Lycan world since before our grandfather was born."

"I had not thought of that, but you are probably right." Before I could question him about Melissa, Victoria came walking up to us on the path.

"Your Highness," She bowed her head.

Grayson nudged me, "Victoria, I am your brother now. Please call me Murdoc," I said, my brother, nodded his approval.

Grayson took Victoria's hand, "Come to dinner tomorrow, brother." And they walked off back toward the lake. I looked up at the sun, it has been hours since I talked to Melissa, and I wondered if she forgot to come out. I headed back to the main compound and stopped when I saw Melissa getting out of her car. She was dressed very differently than she was at the mating ceremony and yesterday at the hospital. Today, she had on a pair of jeans, and a white t-shirt tucked in only in the front. Her brown hair was tied up in a long braid that fell down her back. Not stopping she walked straight up to Lucas' house and knocked on the door.

Lucas saw me when he answered and motioned to me for Melissa to look. She turned her head, and even from this distance, I saw her eyes flash. I closed the distance, and Lucas allowed me entrance. "Melissa is upstairs with Samantha and Aileen." He volunteered.

We both waited until they came down, little Kelvin was playing with his toys on the floor in the family room. "Aileen is just like her father and stubborn, but Melissa suggested I start giving her a bottle of formula and a little cereal to get her to sleep through the night." There was a melancholy tone, "I am going to have to wean her early."

Melissa sensed Samantha's stress, "Not completely, just before she goes to bed. You can get a pump and use your milk to mix with the cereal." Pulling out her phone, she found one online and showed it to Samantha, "This one is highly rated, and I know a couple of the nurses at the hospital have used it."

Samantha cheered up and smiled then she noticed me standing there. "Oh, Your Highness. I am sorry we are talking about such personal things."

"Not to worry," I wanted to put her at ease, "And why don't you call me Murdoc." Now waiting to see what Melissa would do, "Dr. Herbert." I acknowledged her, raising my eyebrow.

There was a sneer on her face at the challenge I just presented her, "Your Highness." She turned to Lucas; "I will email you the link to the pump," Then patting Samantha on the hand, "Let me know if Aileen starts to sleep better."

Then she turned her back to me and walked to the foray. I was right behind her, I reached out and placed my hand around her arm, leaning down to her ear, "We need to talk, Melissa."

My grip was not tight, and she pulled her arm free, "I don't think so, your highness," with a harsh whisper. Then she looked past me back to where Lucas and Samantha were standing watching this exchange. She smiled sweetly then glared up at me. Reaching for the door she walked out, with me on her heels.

I heard Lucas say to Samantha, "They are fated."

Chapter 12

Melissa

Sleep evaded me after I spoke to Murdoc, my mind would not shut down to what his kiss meant, and what the visions were telling me. "Esmee, I need you," I called out to my empty apartment, but she too avoided me. I took a long hot shower and washed my mass of hair, usually, I did this only once a week, because it was not only long but thick, and it was a chore to wash, dry and try to style it in any fashion. After I let it towel dry, I decided to just braid it, and even that took over thirty minutes.

Determined not to go to the compound I decided to sit down and veg out in front of my TV. Another rarity for me. But I was not about to step outside of my apartment with my security detail following me everywhere. If I needed anything I would just order it. The one thing I did relent on was my phone. I turned it back on to make sure the hospital had not called. Thankfully they hadn't, but I did have a voicemail from Lucas. "Melissa this is Lucas, sorry to bother you, but Aileen is not sleeping at night, and I wondered if you could come out and check on her."

I closed my eyes and sighed. I debated what I should do, I could pretend I didn't get the message and not go, but then again. Lucas called me to check on their baby, I could not and would not leave the innocent to continue not to sleep. Returning Lucas' call, "Hey Lucas, I just got your message. I will be out in about an hour to check on her."

"Thank you, Melissa. Why don't you stay for dinner as well."

I had to think quickly, not wanting to be out at the compound longer than necessary, "Thank you, I already have dinner plans." That should work I thought, plans to run through a drive-thru on the way home and veg out in front of the TV as my original plan.

"Okay, we will see you in an hour."

Hefting myself off the sofa, I went into my bedroom and grabbed a pair of sneakers and socks. I was ready in about five minutes, no sense in putting this off, I grabbed my stethoscope and keys and walked out the door, locking it behind me. The whole drive out to the compound my stomach flipped one way then the other over the thought of seeing Murdoc there. I had not bothered to call or text him to say that I was on my way there. I didn't want to see or talk to him. He has made up his mind, he is leaving. And I can't do anything about that.

But somewhere deep inside of me I knew that was a lie, I did want to see him. His gentle kiss last night awakened not only my powers but a stirring in me. I wanted him to want me. Waving at the guard at the gate, I passed through without any trouble and parked in front of Lucas' house. Lucas opened the door at my knock and motioned to Murdoc coming back toward the houses on the path. My heartbeat sped up, and I am pretty sure I started to blush, thankfully Lucas didn't say a thing, because I know he noticed. But trying to play down my feelings, I just shrugged and walked in to greet Samantha holding little Aileen.

We took the baby upstairs, and I examined her, she was a cute little bundle, and happy for any attention. When I picked her up, she turned her head to my breast, laughing, "Sorry little one, I am not your mama." I turned her in my arms and handed her back to her mother. "I think this little one just needs a little more in her bedtime meal. Try adding some cereal to her milk before bedtime. That should get her to sleep longer."

It was hard not to notice the disparity on Samantha's face, but she agreed. And took her daughter from me. When we walked back downstairs, the first thing I saw was Murdoc staring at me as I descended the stairs, but Samantha revealed her distress, she was still nursing and was sad at the fact of weaning her daughter. Understanding, I offered her a solution that I hope would help.

Samantha had not noticed Murdoc until then, and blushing to the roots of her copper curls, bowed her head and addressed him. The gentleman that he was, he put her at ease and offered for her to call him by his given name. Then he addressed me with a cocked eyebrow. I sneered at him but did as he asked before. "Your Highness," turning to leave I told Lucas I would send him the information he needed to get the pump for Samantha and headed straight for the front door patting her hand as I left. Murdoc was right behind me.

Before I could pull the door open, he clutched my arm and whispered that we needed to talk. Pulling my arm free, "I don't think so. Your Highness." Looking behind him Lucas was standing with his arms crossed over his chest grinning, and Samantha looked confused at the exchange between us. Grabbing the door handle and ignoring Murdoc, I stormed out and straight to my car.

"We need to talk." He growled. His hand covered mine, not allowing me to open the driver's door. I knew he would not hurt me, so I pulled my hand free, thinking I could move around him and go in through the passenger door. I pushed him, and he didn't budge, I pushed again, and this time he grinned and shook his head, "That's cute you think you could move me, Melissa."

"It's Doctor Herbert," I seethed.

"We're not at the hospital," he pointed out. Taking my hand, "Either follow along, or I throw you over my shoulder." It was a warning, I believed.

He looked around, stopped, listened for a moment, nodding his head, "Come on." I didn't argue, I had come up with a few things I wanted to say to him as well. He led me between Levi's and Noah's houses and walked up onto the porch. "Sit," he pointed to a chair.

It was only a split second from the time I sat until I jumped back up, starting to pace back and forth. "Why did you kiss me if you are leaving?"

He had propped his hip against the railing but was close enough to the stairs to catch me if I bolted. Shrugging his shoulder, "I wanted to."

Huffing out a breath, "You didn't think it would be more gentlemanly to ask me first?"

The corner of his mouth twitched up, "You think I am a gentleman?"

Turning my back to him I closed my eyes, "This is who I am to be mated with?" I asked the air.

"Who are you talking to?" Murdoc asked.

"No one you know," grinning at my answer.

Running his hand down his face and beard, "We are getting off track." As I paced, he grabbed me, placing his arms on my shoulders he drew me to him, "May I kiss you, Melissa?" It was sweet but I didn't know why.

Shaking my head, "You just can't take liberties, if you are going to leave me."

"Do you think I would not come back for you?" He was pulling me closer.

"Yes. No. I don't know," I whispered. Still, only a step away from him, my body screamed to close the gap.

"You recognized me the moment I stepped up to that mating circle. Just like I recognized you. We are fated, Melissa." He was smiling.

"But you said you are leaving," I pointed out.

Sighing, "I have a clan to run, and things I need to fix before I could bring you there."

Laying my hand on his chest, I closed my eyes, images flashed before me, then I looked again at him, "There are prejudices in your clan."

Tilting his head to the side, "How do you know such things?"

I smiled slightly, "It's a family trait." Reaching up, I ran my fingers through his beard, watching them.

He pulled my hand to his mouth kissing my fingers, then wrapped it around his neck. Lowering his head, his hand clutched the back of my neck and tilted my head as his mouth covered mine. I didn't resist, even closing the step between us. I opened my mouth to him, and his tongue crashed into my mouth. Not shy, my tongue mingled and danced with his.

Wanting this kiss to last forever, I placed my other hand on his heart. Flashes of our life together appeared in my head, the last image, there standing beside Murdoc, the Lycan that killed my parents.

Pushing with all my might, I stepped back. Murdoc was shocked, growling low. "He is with you, the one that killed them."

Stepping further back, he reached out his hand. "Melissa?"

Shaking my head, I put up my hand and screamed, "NO!" I ran down the stairs and around between the houses.

Murdoc was coming around, the corner, when I held out my hand again, screaming so loud that the windows shook in the six houses surrounding me. Lucas emerged from his house, and the others came from the training fields. Holding out my hands, "Leave me be!" I screamed again. This time all of them stopped in their tracks, I could tell I had rendered them frozen in place with just my words, turning I ran to my car, throwing my phone to the ground as I sped out of the compound.

I raced to my apartment and grabbed clothes packing what was within reach, before I raced out the door again, leaving it wide open.

Chapter 13

Murdoc

Not sure what a banshee sounded like, but I think Melissa's screams were close. I stood motionless as I watched Melissa run to her car and leave. It was only a couple of minutes before any of us were able to move again. Looking at Lucas, Samantha had come out of the house clutching their young to her.

Grayson ran out of his house calling out, "What the fuck just happened?"

Lucas turned and whispered in Samantha's ear, then kissed her and each of the babies before she turned back into their house.

Levi, Noah, Wyatt, and Jackson all had gathered. "Murdoc let's take this to Levi's," he walked past.

Nodding, but worried, I pulled my phone from my back pocket and dialed Melissa, it rang on the ground beside where her car had been parked, I walked over and picked it up, putting it in my back pocket. Then walked to Levi's home.

Not waiting for anyone to start, "Lucas, you must tell me now. Why are you protecting Melissa?"

Lucas sighed and nodded, "Melissa is the descendant of my great aunt Esmee. She was a witch that left our grandfather's compound in northern Scotland and traveled to Germany to meet her mate a Lycan clan leader." He let that information sink into all of us, then turned to Levi. "Levi, search for Dr. Melissa Herbert. I don't think you are going to find much, then look for any suspicious Lycan deaths in the United States go back ten years." Levi nodded and walked into another room.

Grayson spoke up, "You think she is a threat to us?"

Lucas shook his head, "No, I think she had a vision when she was speaking with Murdoc, something frightened her."

Finally speaking up, "We weren't exactly talking. But you are right, she pushed away from me and said, *'He is with you. The one that killed them.'* I don't know what she meant."

Lucas nodded, "Melissa; if that is her real name, told me that Esmee cast a spell on her before she died. Her powers were bound, and her Lycan side was laid dormant. Only until she meets and is claimed by her fated mate."

Wyatt spoke up, "Why don't you think that is her real name?"

Before Lucas could answer, Levi came back, "You were right Lucas, there isn't much on Dr. Melissa Herbert. She didn't exist until she entered college. All her transcripts and records are forgeries, good ones but forgeries. I am running a search now on any Lycan deaths."

Lucas turned to Wyatt, "Because I don't know of any Lycan clans with the name of Herbert in them. I am sure they used aliases as well."

He turned his attention to me, "Murdoc, I am sure she meant that she saw the Lycan that killed her parents. Then she saw him again in her vision he is a part of your clan."

Lowering my head, "Do I just leave her alone?" I asked the group gathered but looked at Grayson.

"No, brother. She is your mate, you are destined to be together," he answered, reaching he patted my leg. "We will get this straightened out."

Lucas nodded, "You are her mate and the only one that could awaken her powers, what we saw today is just a taste of what she can do." Stopping for a moment, "I think I have letters from Esmee in the corridor to my grandmother, they may provide us with some information."

Noah had been listening to the conversation, all the while looking at his phone, "There were a group of Lycan witch hunters that came out of Ireland in the 1400s. It was believed that all had been caught and persecuted for their crimes. But not, if one is in your clan." He handed his phone over to Levi, so he could investigate it further.

Looking at my brother, "I need to find her."

Grayson nodded, and Lucas spoke up, "We are going to. Her powers are rising, and she needs more protection the ever." Looking at Grayson, "We three will go."

"Levi, you keep searching," Lucas was in his element of being a commander. "Noah, Jax, Wyatt, you three see if there is any damage to any of the buildings and start repairs if needed. We'll be back as soon as we can."

Grayson and I stood and exited Levi's house. Grayson wanted to lighten my mood, "That must have been some kiss." He walked off toward the barn.

Lucas heard him and chuckled as he walked over to his home. "I'm just going to tell Samantha where we are going."

Chapter 14

Melissa

They will find me soon; I used my credit card to get this room at this little motel. I was sitting on the side of the bed, looking down at my hands, they shook still. I had rendered them all motionless. "What did I do?"

"You are coming into your powers," Esmee said in my head.

Shaking my head, "I could have killed them." Tears were streaming down my face.

"No. You intended to get them to not follow you. Your heart and words were not deadly." Her voice was calming but was not helping my despair.

I paced for an hour or so until exhaustion took over and I finally laid down on the bed closing my eyes. Peaceful visions played out in my mind. Children, boys, and girls playing in fields of flowers. Murdoc was standing at my side watching them with a smile on his face.

"He is coming," Esmee called out in my head. Raising my arm, I looked at my watch, I had been asleep for several hours.

Swinging my legs over the bed, I walked to the door, pulling it open just as Murdoc was about to knock.

I bowed my head, "Your Highness." Then stepped back. Grayson and Lucas stood behind him. "You might as well come in too." I swung my arm wide. "This place is not much for entertaining, but..." I shrugged my shoulders.

Murdoc's eyes flashed red, as he stalked in grabbing the door and swinging it shut on Lucas and Grayson. Nearly running backward, I stopped when my back hit the wall. His one hand was braced against the wall as his other reached out and pushed back a strand of hair that had come loose from my braid, "Are you okay?" he whispered.

At first, I nodded then changed to a shake, "I am fine. I didn't hurt anyone did I?" My eyes were looking straight at his. "I could not live with myself if I hurt someone." I felt a tear trailing down my cheek.

Still being tender, "You didn't hurt anyone, we just could not move for a few minutes." Sighing, "You need to tell me everything, Melissa."

There was a knock on the door, and Grayson opened it. "Hate to break up you lovers..." He smiled at Murdoc's growl. "But Lucas wants to get back to the compound."

Afraid of what could happen, "I can't go back there. I am a danger to all of you." If I could have, I would back up further into the wall.

Murdoc turned and looked at his brother, "We will be out in a moment." Then he turned back to me, "Walk or over my shoulder?"

Shaking my head, "Please, Murdoc. Think of the little ones."

Reaching down he took my hand and placed it on his heart, "I won't let you hurt anyone. Especially the little ones."

That made me smile, "How would you stop me?"

A low growl came from him, as he lowered his head capturing my mouth in a long kiss. I focused only on him and blocked out the visions that were trying to intrude. Lost in Murdoc's embrace, moments passed, then another knock came on the door, and Murdoc lifted his head with an arrogant satisfied grin on his face. "Walk or over my shoulder?" He asked again.

"I'll walk, thank you." I mocked stepping around him. As he passed the dresser, he grabbed the bag I had packed, then opened the door for me.

Lucas was standing just outside looking grim, while Grayson was grinning like a fool. "Melissa," Lucas nodded and turned on his heel toward a black SUV that was parked close to the office. Grayson slid into the driver's seat, Lucas in the passenger, and Murdoc held the back seat door open for me to get in. Then he walked around climbing in beside me and tossed my bag into the cargo area.

The drive felt like it took forever, the tension in the SUV was thick. I knew they wanted to talk, and I didn't know where to start. "I'm sorry. I didn't mean to ..."

Lucas interrupted me, "Melissa, you are coming into your powers, no apologies are necessary."

I had lowered my head, and Murdoc reached over covering my clasped hands with his. Looking up at him, all I could manage was a weak smile. We pulled up into the compound, and Lucas called over to several of the trainees. "Get the cargo truck and go to Melissa's. Clean out her apartment." Turning to me, "We locked your door when we went looking for you," it was a statement.

Before I could open my mouth to argue, I realized he was right. I had used my powers, and witch hunters would start looking for me. I pulled my keyring out of my pocket and handed it to Murdoc. He tossed them to Lucas and wrapped his arm around me.

Samantha came out of her house and ran up to swallow me up in a hug, "We were so worried about you." I looked up to see Victoria standing on their porch, smiling at me as well.

"I'm sorry," whispering to her, "I didn't mean to ..." I broke off in a sob.

"Hush," Samantha soothed, "Everyone is fine. I am just thankful they were able to find you." Her hands were running up and down my back as she continued to soothe my tears.

Calming, I whispered, "Is he still behind me?"

I could feel her chuckle, "Yes." Nodding I straightened up and turned around. Samantha just stepped around me, and patted Murdoc's chest, "Sometimes us females just need a good cry." His eyes furrowed, as he looked down at her and then back up at me. I went from sobbing one minute to giggling the next. "See, she is all better."

Turning to walk back to her house, Samantha called over her shoulder just before she opened the door, "Victoria and I are cooking for everyone this evening. Dinner is at eight. Don't be late." Then they both disappeared behind the door.

"A good cry?" Murdoc was still frowning at me.

Nodding my head, "Yes, it is a good stress reliever, you should try it sometime." Looking around Lucas and Grayson had disappeared. Taking my hand, he led me over to the training fields. I watched as each of his security lined up at his command, "Do you see him?" His tone was deadly.

With a shake of my head, I murmured, "No."

Satisfied, Murdoc spoke up, "This is Melissa. She is my mate; you will protect her as you do me." Each one, in turn, came before me and knelt, "Your Highness, I swear fealty to you, to protect and serve you and to defend you against every creature with all my power until I depart this earth." Murdoc nodded to each as they stood satisfied.

"Why did they just do that?" whispering as I blushed to my toes. "And I am not 'Your Highness' you are.

Murdoc looked to his men, "Carry on," then took my hand. "You are my mate, that makes you Princess of Arcadia. You will have to get used to being addressed formally."

We walked over to Levi's, Murdoc knocked on the door, and we walked in after Lucas answered. Just looking at the seriousness of these six faces, I was a bundle of nerves again. Murdoc squeezed my hand. "Melissa, what is your real name?" Lucas asked.

"Melissa is my real first name, in German it is Melisse. My last name is Mueller." Answering, sitting straighter. We came to the United States when I was four, my parents took the name of Brenner at first, then when I went to school, I changed it to Herbert."

All of them nodded, and Levi said, "That will make my search easier." Then left the room.

Murdoc looked at me, "Can you tell us what you remember of the night they died?"

Nodding I looked down at Murdoc's hand still holding mine, "My mother contacted me and insisted I come home for a weekend."

Lucas, "She called you?"

I looked up at him, "No," I taped my head, "Telepathically." Smiling at their shocked faces, "We had always been able to communicate that way since I was a child. It drove my father crazy."

"Go on," Lucas urged.

With a glance at Murdoc, he nodded, "Both of my parents were agitated when I got home. She had seen the witch hunter getting closer to them. Wanting to hide me further from him she put a charm on me so I would not smell like a witch." Wiping away the tear, "It was that spell that drew him to her." Stopping for a minute to take some quick breaths, "I had walked to my car to put some of my belongings in it, I was returning and close to the house, when I heard my mother scream. Then I saw the flames, and my father let out a loud growl. Then nothing."

"You didn't go back in the house?" Wyatt asked.

Shaking my head, "No, Esmee stopped me." Tears were falling, "she told me they were dead, and I should run. But I waited and watched."

"That's when you saw him?" Murdoc asked.

I looked at my hands then back into his eyes, "Yes. He came out of the house and sniffed, but he could not smell me. My mother's charm worked." Looking over to Grayson, "That is why when I was here treating Victoria, none of you could smell that I am a witch."

Lucas added, "Only until I saw your eyes change." I nodded.

There was a light tap on the door, and Victoria's voice rang out, "Dinner is ready. And you are late."

Grayson shook his head, and stood, "We better not make them wait any longer," Stretching, "And I am hungry."

We filed out the door, and to Lucas and Samantha's house, where they had set up a buffet-type meal for an army. Unlike Grayson, I wasn't hungry but was not going to be impolite, so I put small amounts of each dish on my plate before carrying it out the French doors and sat on the steps looking out to the forest beyond.

Forcing myself to take a few bites of food, was all I could manage. I was terrified of what I had done earlier today. Closing my eyes, I could see Murdoc in the house, talking to Grayson and Levi, but his eyes never left my back. Victoria crossed my vision and came out sitting beside me.

"I understand," she offered. "When I woke up and started to change, I was terrified."

Looking over to her, "What did you do?"

With a smile, "I am still doing it," she said. "I go out to the lake and meditate, every morning." With a shrug, "You can come with me tomorrow if you like." Then she smiled and stood, "Not hungry?" she pointed to my plate lying on the porch beside my hip.

I shook my head, "No, not really. It was delicious though." She reached out her hand, and I lifted my plate to her.

As she walked through the French doors, Murdoc held it open for her letting her pass. Then he sat beside me. "You didn't eat much, doctor," uttered nudging my shoulder.

The smile I gave him was weak at best, I'm not hungry," continuing, "Victoria said she meditates, and it helps her with all the changes." I didn't want him to leave, but I wasn't sure what to say so I blurted out the only thing I could think of.

He thought for a moment, "Why not try it," he offered. "Could help you get control of your powers." Standing up, he walked down the three steps then turned and offered me his hand, "Let's walk out to the lake."

Chapter 15

Murdoc

Melissa was quiet and withdrawn when we came in to eat. I watched as she made a plate of bits and pieces of food, then walked out to sit alone on the porch. Stuck between Grayson and Levi having a debate about how to flush out the witch hunter in my clan, I watched each time her fork was raised to her mouth. The two were still debating on the best course of action, but my eyes stayed on her, it was strange, but I could feel her watching me, even though her back was facing me.

When I saw Victoria go out and speak with her, then she stood to come back in, this was my chance, mumbling, "Excuse me." I moved to the French doors, holding it open for Victoria.

Victoria whispered as she passed me, "She hardly ate a thing."

My eyes darted to the plate she held in her hand, and even though I knew her fork went to her mouth five times, Victoria was right, she barely ate a thing. As I stepped out and sat beside her, I teased her about not eating, her response was just above a whisper. She was still troubled about what had happened that afternoon. Then she mentioned Victoria meditating, I thought for a moment and agreed it could help her. At least I don't think it would hurt. I stood and held out my hand to her, suggesting we take a walk to the lake.

Her blue eyes looked up at me, and then at my hand. I didn't rush her, just waited for her to make up her mind. She reached out her hand and placed it in mine, and I helped her stand. Not wanting to break the contact, I didn't let go and shortened my stride so that she didn't have to run to keep up with me. We didn't speak as we walked, I just held back any branches that were in our path, as I continued to lead her to the lake.

Once we got to the grassy spot facing the water I sat and leaned back against a tree, one leg was extended, and my knee was up. Melissa stood still for a moment then walked to the edge of the water. "It's probably freezing this time of year," I called out, just watching her.

I heard her take a deep calming breath and folded her hands in front of her, then her voice rang out in my head, *"Did you know that Lucas' grandmother and my aunt Noémie could talk to Callen telepathically?"* She didn't move.

"No," I thought. *"I barely knew her before she died."*

"Oh," Her voice called out in my head.

"Were you watching me in the house?" I asked.

"Yes, how did you know?" she responded.

"I felt you." Answering back. "Come here, Melissa," I called out my demand.

She turned and looked at me, her eyes had changed to the most purist blue I had ever seen. Walking to me, she said, "Seems our connection is strong too."

When she was within reach, I sat forward and pulled her down between my legs with her back to my chest. Wrapping my arms around her I could feel her heart beating against my chest. "It would seem so." I inhaled her scent, "Is your scent still masked from me?"

She turned her head some, "Yes," taking another deep breath, I heard her mumbling in German. "Inhale now." She said after a moment.

The combination of scents filled my soul, sage, with a fruity hint of citrus and the woods. "This is you?" She nodded.

"Only you will be able to smell me, until..." She didn't finish.

I held her tighter, "I understand." I kissed the side of her neck inhaling her again. "You smelled like vanilla and jasmine before."

She chucked, "My body wash."

Lying her head back on my shoulder, we stayed silent for a time. When she finally spoke, "Murdoc, I am afraid."

"Of me?" I asked, turning my head to look at her.

Her eyes glistened with tears, "No, of what is to come after you claim me." Before I could reassure her, "And I am afraid for you."

Cupping her chin I turned her face to me, "No tears," whispering, she turned in my lap and I kissed each of her eyes. "We will get through this. You can see the future, tell me, have you seen my death?"

She shook her head, "I can't tell you the future, I have been warned."

Leaning closer to her, "Tell grandma to close her eyes, I am going to kiss you."

She smiled, "She heard you." Her hand came up around my neck as the other lay on my heart.

My fingers threaded into the braid at the back of her neck holding her still as I started to ravage her mouth. Melissa was not a timid participant; her tongue was just as needy as mine. Not happy with our positions, I held her tight as I flipped her over onto her back. Sitting back on my knees, I stripped off my shirt and tossed it to the right. Her eyes flashed blue looking at me, then I reached for her t-shirt and pulled it up over her head, it landed on top of mine, then she sat up, reached behind her, and when her bra come loose, I pulled the straps down her arms, and away from her perfect body. "You are flawless, not a mark on you."

Her hand reached out and her fingers trailed over my chest, "I heal, like you. Half Lycan. Remember."

My beast was restless, as I leaned down claiming her mouth again. *Ours!* My beast howled.

Moving down her neck, "Yes I am yours" she muttered. I smiled, she had heard my beast, as I continued to her breast.

Taking her nipple in my mouth, she gasped with surprise and then moaned with pleasure.

"You are so responsive to us," I growled, moving from one breast to the other. "I'm going to make you cum, Melissa." I looked up into her eyes. She smiled and nodded, "You understand?"

She smiled and rolled her eyes, "I may be a virgin, but I am a doctor, Murdoc. Yes, I know what you mean," a little exasperated.

I grasped both of her hands in mine, pulling them up over her head, and held them still, demanding. "Say my name again."

Her eyes widened as she obeyed, "Murdoc," she moaned.

"Such sweet lips," I growled. "They are going to look beautiful wrapped around my cock when we mate." Again, her eyes widened for just a moment, then she licked her lips. "You like the fantasy I put in your head."

Rising just a bit she rubbed her nipples against the hair on my chest, as she moaned, "I do."

My eyes glowed down at her, "Such an imp you are, Melissa. I am going to have to teach you some manners." Her eyes dilated as she smiled.

Moving away from her, I wanted to see if she would obey my commands. Offering her my hand I helped her up, "Take off your pants for me," demanding.

Her eyes flashed first with anger then excitement, as she slowly moved her hands to the waistband of her jeans. Then stepping closer to me, she braced a hand on my shoulder so she could remove her shoes. Then she stepped back and lowered her jeans, kicking them to the side. Her breathing was heavy, excited about what I would do next.

Not moving, I took my time looking at her perfect body with only a thin thong hiding in between her ass cheeks. When I came around behind her, I ran my fingers down her arms, watching as the goosebumps formed under my touch. "I want you only to think of me, and what I am doing to you, Melissa."

She nodded, "Not good enough," I slapped her ass. "Say the words."

"Yes." Whispering.

Another crack of my hand on her ass, "No," I cooed in her ear, "Yes, what?"

She spun her face to look at me, gritting her teeth, "Sir?"

Shaking my head, "No," I cooed again, "Your..." I coaxed.

"Highness." She breathed out.

Rubbing my hand over the red prints I made on her ass, "Now your thong, take it off."

She did as she was commanded, but before she could toss it to the side, I held out my hand, and gently she placed it in my palm. Bringing it to my nose I inhaled the arousal that was permeating from them, then slipped the garment into my pocket.

I was not sure when she shivered or if it was from cold or arousal, but I was not done with her. I left her standing there, and moved back to my spot at the tree, leaning back, "Come to me, Melissa." I reached out my hand, as she stepped forward, laying her hand in mine.

With one swift move, I pulled her down over my lap, and slapped her bare ass again, "Never again, will you use your powers against me."

She tried to rear up away from me, but I was too strong for her. Another slap, "You will not sit down for a week but trying to get away from me. Now say the words."

"Yes, Your Highness." Uttering.

Rubbing the handprint, I had just made, I moved my hand to the crest of her buttocks then followed the seam, down to her core. "Open your legs for me."

She did what she was told, and sliding my finger into her, she was wet with arousal. "My little doctor enjoys being disciplined."

"Yes, Your Highness," she moaned as I moved my finger in and out of her imitating the fucking ritual.

With each thrust of my finger, she became wetter, lifting her, I turned her and laid her back down on her back. Spreading her legs wide, I moved down her body until my beard grazed over her clit. "You smell so good, Melissa. Are you ready to cum for me?"

Moaning with pleasure and anticipation, "Yes, Your Highness."

"Good girl," I praised just before I dove into the feast of what was awaiting me between her legs. She was already drenched, and her juices flowed all over my beard. Taking her clit in between my teeth, I gave her a little more pain, but I could tell by the way she held my head to her cunt, she was in ecstasy.

Moving my hand, I slid my finger back into her body, fucking her. Reaching the barrier of her virginity, I didn't push through, not yet. That was all mine too, but only on the next full moon. She was on the verge of an orgasm, but I wanted her all night, so I pulled back.

The purest of blue eyes looked up at me, and she pouted. I chuckled and moved up beside her, moving her so that her back was to my chest, I pulled her leg up over my hip and trailed my fingers down her stomach. Reaching down further, I lightly smacked her exposed clit with my hand, "Your pouting is adorable, but only for when we are like this." I emphasized my point by giving her another slap.

Moaning, her head fell back to my shoulder, as she reached down to hold my hand to her core. "Murdoc please," She begged.

"Say my name again," I demanded rubbing my thumb over her clit.

"Murdoc," she moaned. Her body was growing tighter, and I knew she was closer to the edge now. Sliding my finger back into her as my thumb continued to rub her clit. "Please," she begged again.

I realized she was holding back until I permitted her to cum. "Now, my sweet," I whispered into her ear. She let go, and her cunt convulsed over my finger, even her body shook with her orgasm. My movements slowed to bring her down, I felt when she relaxed against me and fell asleep. I moved slowly to my back, and in her sleep, she draped herself over my chest.

Chapter 16

The sun was cresting over the eastern horizon when I opened my eyes. Murdoc had his arm around me, holding me close to him. When I tried to move, his arm tightened. "I'm sorry I didn't mean to wake you."

"No apologies necessary," he smiled. Then he looked up at the sky, "But I do need to get you back before my security or Lucas comes looking for you." He stood and grabbed his t-shirt laying on the ground, "Put that on." Tossing it to me.

Pulling his shirt over my head, I held out my hand, "May I please have back my thong?"

A wide grin came across his face as he shook his head, "No, those belong to me now." I watched as he pulled them from his pocket and brought them to his face again, "The scent of your nectar is all over them." Then he shoved them back down into his pocket.

My phone rang, and he pulled it from his back pocket and handed it to me. Looking down, it was the hospital calling. "I'm late for work." I showed him the screen.

He stilled my hand, "You're not going to work, Melissa." His voice was stern, and I knew he was right.

"This is Dr. Herbert," I answered. "Oh, I am sorry, I had a family emergency and had to leave town late last night." I looked at Murdoc as his eyebrow shot up an inch at my lie. I listened for a moment, "Again, I am sorry, I will call HR when they open and put in for my vacation time." Pausing to listen as I was chastised on the other end. "Yes, it will never happen again." Then I hung up. "I probably just lost my job," I uttered.

"You used your powers yesterday. I will not let you take a chance on your safety." He had wrapped his arms around me, holding me tight, almost like he was afraid of losing me. My shoulders slumped but I knew he was right.

Moving against him I started to pick up my clothes, then looked up at him, "I can't go back to Lucas' with only your shirt on."

"You are not going back to Lucas'," Seeing the confused look on my face, "You are staying with me until I fly home, then you will be staying with Lucas and Samantha." Opening my mouth to protest, he put his fingers to my lips and shook his head, "No arguments, Melissa. This is my command." His eyes flashed and by the time he finished, he was growling.

He reached down and handed me my shoes. Then swung me up in his arms. "Besides, no one gets to see your body but me."

Laying my head on his shoulder, "Possessive much?" I uttered.

But of course, he heard me, "With you, always." He carried me back to Noah's house and went in through the back. Taking the steps two at a time he opened the door to a bedroom and laid me in the middle of the bed, then turned and locked the door. Stripping out of his jeans, he was gloriously nude.

There wasn't an ounce of fat on him, I saw him shirtless last night and was amazed at the muscles that rippled down his abdomen. The tattoo on his chest was of a Celtic cross. Now, his cock stood straight from his body hard, long, and thick. I must have licked my lips staring at him because I heard him chuckle. "Are you done with your inspection, doctor?" My eyes had not left his cock as I nodded. I jumped when he lifted me to pull back the covers, then put me back in the bed, "Roll over on your side."

Blushing to the roots of my hair, I did as he said, then I felt the mattress move when he climbed in behind me. "You know I can see you in my mind."

"Do you want another spanking?" He grumbled, rubbing my bare ass with his hand. "Go to sleep, Melissa. We will mate on the next full moon, after that, you can have me whenever you want."

My eyes closed, but the visions returned, one moment Murdoc was standing beside me smiling at our children, the next he was chained to a wall. An axe was propped not far from him. "Melissa, wake up." It was Murdoc. "You're dreaming."

I turned in his arms and wept. "No, they are not dreams. You can't go back there."

"Shhh, Melissa. I must, for your safety." He whispered to the top of my head; I just shook my head because I knew I could not tell him about my visions of the future. Soon I fell back to sleep, this time peacefully.

When I woke again, Murdoc was gone, he had left my bag on a chair and opened the door to an adjoining bathroom. I showered and dressed, slowly coming down the stairs. Samantha and Victoria were waiting for me, "Tea or coffee?" Victoria asked.

Blushing "Coffee please." Then I looked around for Murdoc.

"He's out with Lucas and Grayson." Samantha offered, "They are making plans for your safety while you are here."

"They are going to lock down the compound," Victoria added.

"It isn't me I am worried about." I lowered my head.

Samantha reached out, "What is it, Melissa? You can tell us."

Sniffing back the tears that were threatening to flow, "I can't. I have been warned not to tell anyone about my visions."

Victoria tilted her head, "Warned from who?"

"Esmee, I would assume," Lucas' voice came from the doorway.

Looking at his wife, "They are down for their nap, I can hear them."

Coming back to the conversation, "What is she afraid will happen if you talk about your visions?" It was Victoria.

Sighing, Lucas produced a bundle of letters and journals, "Because, from the small amount I read, Noémie and Esmée's mother was hung then burned alive by a human that claimed her to be a witch."

"My God," "That's horrible," Samantha and Victoria said at the same time.

Lucas smiled, "She was telling him the future, and he was becoming rich from the information, but she saw something and stopped." Holding out his hand with the bundle, "You read them, Melissa, I think they may help you."

"I can't take those from you, they belong to your grandmother." I shook my head.

"And yours," he laid them in front of me, "There are letters from Esmee to my grandmother, read them."

Gingerly, I reached out my hand, "I will return them when I am done." Lucas moved over toward me and kissed me on top of my head like a child.

There was a growl that came from behind him, giggling, I look up at his face, "You did that on purpose." Pulling away, he winked at me.

He turned to leave, "Your Highness." Uttering as he bowed his head.

Murdoc strode in, unhappy with Lucas, "What are those?" he asked pointing to the bundle.

"Letters from Esmee and Noémie's journals. Lucas thought they may give me some answers by reading them." I explained.

Grumbling, he took my coffee cup from my hands and drank the rest. Then leaning close to my ear, "No one kisses you but me, Imp."

Lowering my head, "Yes, Your Highness." I whispered back blushing, because Samantha and Victoria were still there, watching our exchange.

"Good Girl," He praised against my ear, then poured me another cup of coffee from the pot. Setting it down in front of me before he turned to leave again.

As soon as the door closed behind him, "Spill!" they both said.

Trying to stand, I reached for the bundle, "I really should start reading these."

Samantha's hand laid on top of the letters, "Not until you tell us what that was all about."

"You sounded submissive," Victoria's grin was wide.

"We or he did things to me last night." I admitted, "and I liked it."

My face was hot from blushing, "What things?" Samantha grinned. Victoria was just as eager to hear.

Looking around, "He spanked me. And demanded I call him 'Your Highness'." I blurted out. These two were relentless to get the information out of me, and I finally told them everything. It felt nice to have girlfriends I could confide in.

After they left, I took that packet of letters and journals up to the room Murdoc and I shared. First, I straightened up, and then sat in a chair and began to read.

Noémie's journals started with when and how she met Callen, Lucas' grandfather. She wrote that not only had her mother been telling the human about the future, but she had fallen in love with him, it was when she saw a vision of him marrying another woman that she stopped giving him the information he demanded. Then warned Noémie that she should never tell anyone what she sees in her visions, it was too dangerous. It followed their journey and then finally the perilous trip to Wick, Scotland. I cried when she talked about how she nearly died.

Her journal continued and she even wrote that after Esmee left, she started to tell Callen about her visions, but she never would tell him bad things to come. *'Sharing my visions with Callen is a relief from carrying a burden. But the vision I had today, I will not tell him, it would crush him to know our Patrick is going to perish soon. I am trying to hold back my tears now, and I know this will not happen for some years to come.'*

Then she went on, *'Esmee left us today. Her journey will be long and hard. Witch hunters are everywhere in that part of the world. But I know she will find him. She said that she has traveled through an eagle and had already met him some weeks ago."*

'I tried today sitting out by the brook to mind-link with a sparrow that was nesting in a nearby tree. But was unable to connect to it. I am a little disappointed that I too didn't inherit this power, only Esmee.'

Putting the journal down, I wandered out to the lake, sitting with my legs crossed, I found a squirrel scampering around. Calming my breathing, and focusing on the animal, my sight changed, and I could see and touch what she was doing. I was not sure how I knew the animal was female, but I did. When a twig snapped behind me, I came up on my hind legs, through the squirrel's eyes I saw Murdoc walking up behind me. I could feel the animals' fear. Murdoc shook me, "Melissa!" called out.

My head fell forward, and the connection was lost. It took me a minute to come back to myself, and when I did Murdoc had his arms around me holding me. "I did it." Whispering.

"You scared the hell out of me! What did you do?" He grumbled holding me tighter.

"Noémie wrote that Esmee was able to animal-link, and she had traveled hundreds of miles and met her mate, long before she ever left Scotland," explaining. "And I was able to link with a squirrel across the lake just now." I was smiling up at him, and he was frowning down at me.

Not letting go, "I should bare your arse right now and spank you until you can't sit down for a week for scaring me like that."

"I don't understand. I didn't use my power against you. I was trying something new." I wiggled to turn and face him.

Taking a calming breath, "You didn't hear me calling you. Your eyes were looking at nothing, it was like you were dead."

Laying my hand on his chest, "I am sorry. I didn't mean to frighten you." Raising my hand, I trailed my fingers through his beard, "Will a kiss make it better?" I smiled trying to lighten his mood.

"What if I could not have woken you from your trance?" He asked.

Lowering my head, "I think that maybe you would be the only one who could wake me." I lowered my hand to his heart and laid my head on his shoulder. "Murdoc, I am going to have to use my powers to get used to them and learn how to control them." I was trying to make him understand that there are things I am going to have to do on my own.

'I don't want to leave you.' I heard his thought.

'I don't want you to go.' I said back. He pulled me back and looked into my eyes, "You hear my thoughts?" I nodded.

"It could be convenient to have a conversation we didn't want anyone else hearing." Shrugging. "Like this morning, Samantha and Victoria heard our conversation."

"Were you embarrassed I called you an 'Imp'?" His grin didn't look like he was sorry.

"Yes and no," honestly. "But those two wouldn't let the subject drop until I told them everything."

"You're pouting again, you know what happens when you pout." He leaned closer to my face. Then pulling back, "You are right, those conversations are for us privately. What did you tell them?" He was grinning again.

"Everything," I uttered, "and that I liked it."

Pulling me to his chest, "You loved it, Imp." Then he kissed the top of my head, before lifting me off his lap. "I am leaving the day after tomorrow. You will stay here under Lucas' protection. And will do as you are told, Understood."

"Yes." I could not help the fear in my voice. Not for myself but for him. He took my hand, and we walked back to the compound, straight to Grayson and Victoria's home.

Our dinner was enjoyable, and Grayson and Murdoc kept the conversation about growing up together, Victoria was giving me sideways glances, and smiling. *'I wish I had not told her a thing.'* I thought, but Murdoc didn't reply, just reached under the table, and squeezed my leg letting me know he heard me.

When we left, we headed straight to Lucas' "I'm not staying with you?" I asked. Lucas had opened the door.

'I am not a saint, Melissa. I can't have your beautiful bare ass up against my nuts again without making you mine tonight." He thought.

"Hello Lucas," I greeted him. *'I wouldn't mind if we went out to the lake right now.'* I replied to Murdoc.

"Lucas," Murdoc greeted him. *'Behave Imp'* he said to me.

Lucas motioned us in, telling me Samantha was upstairs with the children. I walked up the stairs quietly in case the little ones were asleep and peeked into the nursery. "Sleeping?" I whispered.

Samantha nodded and stood from the rocking chair she was in with Aileen, placing her baby in her crib, kissing as she tucked the baby in, then leaned over her son and did the same.

Backing out of the room, she shut the door and motioned for me to follow her. Opening a door at the end of the hall, "This is your room," She opened the door, and there was my bedroom furniture all in place, "I wanted you to feel at home," she uttered.

Turning to her, "Samantha, Thank you." I hugged her.

We walked down the stairs, Lucas was with Murdoc in his office, and the moment he saw me, he closed his mind to me. I understood they were talking about my safety, but it still hurt to think he would not allow me in.

Standing he walked me to the front porch, "Tomorrow I will select the security that will stay with you here." I just nodded.

"Can we talk later?" I looked over my shoulder, I knew Lucas could hear us even through the door. *'I have seen things. I want to tell you about.'* I thought, looking up into his eyes.

'I thought that was forbidden.' He answered.

"Maybe not from what I have read so far in Noémie's journal." I didn't bother thinking about it.

Pulling me to his chest, "Or you could just call me." He smiled.

"Phones are traceable." I smiled.

"Okay, give me an hour." He whispered against my lips, I didn't hesitate, opening my mouth for him. I wanted him. And the more I thought about it, waiting for him to claim me was not what I had in mind.

Chapter 17

Murdoc

When Melissa went upstairs with Samantha, Lucas offered me a chair in his study. "We will lock down the compound as soon as you leave for the airport." He looked me straight in the eye. "Melissa is your mate, but also my family, I will not let anything happen to her."

I nodded. "Her powers are growing."

"You can talk to each other with your minds." He smiled at the knowledge.

"How did you know?" I asked.

"You both are going to have to learn to control your facial expressions." He sat back in his chair, grinning, "My grandparents could do the same, and had the same problem in the beginning."

"She can link to animals, see and feel what they do?" I wasn't sure why I was telling him this. We both heard Samantha and Melissa coming down the stairs. I shook my head 'no' to Lucas, and he understood, I didn't want Melissa to know what we were saying. I cleared my mind, and pretty sure Lucas did the same.

The look on her face told me she knew exactly what I had done. She walked me out and asked to speak to me, she wanted to tell me about some of the visions she had seen. I walked over to Noah's and spoke to him for a few minutes before I went upstairs. Looking around, she had cleaned the room, *"You don't have to clean up after me"* I thought.

"It's a long habit, not because of you. I always keep my room clean." She replied. *"I'm in the tub, give me a little time to get dressed."*

The image of her in the tub popped into my head and instantly I was hard. Not tired, I stripped out of my T-shirt and sat in the chair, waiting for her to talk to me again. Time ticked by, and I looked at my phone, nearly thirty minutes passed since she told me she was in the tub. *"Murdoc, I am at the lake. Please come,"* her voice rang out in my head.

Nearly toppling over the chair when I jumped up, how in the hell did she get out of Lucas' house without him hearing? Not bothering with my shirt, I went downstairs and out the back, straight to the lake, *"I am going to bare your ass for this, Imp,"* I growled in my head.

She didn't reply, that scared the hell out of me. I came to a complete stop when I saw her. She was nude, standing at the edge of the water, the rich brown waves of her hair fell down her back stopping just at her waist. She didn't turn to face me, just stood still. *"I am yours, Murdoc. I don't want to wait, claim me tonight, please."*

Stepping closer to her, "It isn't our tradition." Her head slightly turned, and I could see her eyes were pure crystal blue.

A slight smile played on her mouth. "Do you always follow traditions?"

The hair on my chest brushed against her back I was so close to her now, "Not always." I whispered in her ear. "Why do you want me to claim you now, and not wait?" I had a feeling it was more than just the arousal I could smell from her.

She lowered her head, "You will break the spell Esmee placed on me if you claim me. And I could protect myself with my powers." She wasn't lying or trying to be coy. "But mostly, I keep seeing you in my head this morning standing there nude. You are magnificent by the way."

Up until this point I had not touched her, I knew if I did, I would give her what she wanted. I would claim her this night. Still resisting the urge to touch her, "How did you get out of Lucas' without him or Samantha hearing you?"

"I chanted *'Don't let them hear me.'* Over and over until I was out the French doors in the woods," She answered, then pointing to a garment on the ground. "I was wearing my robe until I got here." She had read my thoughts about the possibility of anyone seeing her running nude across the compound. "Murdoc, please touch me," she uttered her plea.

"If I do, I won't be able to stop." Still, just a breath away from her, I could see her pulse beating in her neck. She was excited, and so aroused.

When she stepped to turn, "Stay where you are, Imp." I commanded.

She lowered her head, "Yes, Your Highness." Those sweet words she just murmured went straight to my cock, remarkably getting harder and bobbing in my jeans.

With my left hand, I grabbed her hair at the base of her neck pulling her head back. "You will learn to obey me, Melissa." Growling in her ear, she didn't cry out, from the little bit of pain I was causing her. Tilting her head exposing her neck, and letting my fangs out, I scrapped them over the sensitive skin, then licked her where she would be wearing my mark by sunrise. She moaned with pleasure but didn't say a word.

Letting go, I stepped back, "Turn around." Doing as she was told, but leaving her head lowered, "Look me in the eye." As I commanded her my eyes were on her breasts watching as they rose and fell with each breath she took, when I looked up and into her eyes they were pure lapis blue. "By all the gods you are beautiful."

Closing her eyes just for the briefest of seconds, she bowed her head, "Thank you, Your Highness," and then reopened her eyes directly into mine.

Raising my hand out to her, "Come to me." She didn't hesitate to lay her hand in mine stepping toward me until her breasts were up against my chest. With my other hand with two fingers under her chin, I raised her face to mine, "Are you ready to be mine, Melissa?" Nodding, she opened her mouth, to respond. As she did, I lowered my head capturing her mouth, delving deep with my tongue. She moaned with pleasure, grasping my arms to hold herself upright. My beast, growled, *"Claim her, she is ours!"*

Wrapping my arms around her I pulled her up and against me. The swollen meat of my cock pulsed against the confines of my jeans. In one swift move, I laid her down on the soft grass and quickly stripped out of my boots and jeans. Once released my cock stood long and hard. "Do you want to stop, Melissa?"

"No," she whispered, but her eyes were wide as she looked at the dense thickness of me.

My hand traveled down my body to wrap around my throbbing shaft. "Watch me," I commanded as I started to pump the hardness. An orgasm was quick to rise, and I growled low and deep as jets of my semen fell over her stomach and breasts. Coming down on my knees, I took her hand, and ran her fingers through the stickiness, then brought it to her lips, "Taste me."

Opening her mouth, I watched as I fed her, licking and sucking. "Now let me watch as you take the rest. She moved her hand repeatedly swiping up my semen and bringing it to her mouth, my cock was hard again, at the site. "Those sweet lips are good for more than kissing, Imp," I growled. Taking her hand, I brought her up, with her face close to the tip, "Open your mouth, and I will teach you how to pleasure me."

She did and learned quickly, grasping my shaft she pumped as she sucked. She even moved so she could be in a better position. As I watched her mouth on my cock. "I knew that would be a beautiful site." Closing my eyes, and leaning back my head, I took pleasure from her mouth and, was nearing my orgasm. "I am going to cum, Melissa. Don't waste a drop, Imp." I smiled as her eyes looked up at me and she nodded. I held her head still as I pumped the last few strokes in her mouth, then filled her throat with semen, obeying my command, she sucked every drop down.

With a gentle hand, I pushed her back down on her back, "Now spread your legs wide." Again, she obeyed without hesitation, I looked down to her folds and clit that glistened with her arousal, then I moved down pushing her legs wider, "Now my turn," first I scrapped my tongue over her clit. "Melissa, remember to ask permission."

"Yes, Your Highness," she moaned out.

Her hard clit was throbbing for release, and I knew it would not take me long to have her begging to let her cum. I smiled up at her and kissed the skin just above her folds, then letting my tongue once again graze over her clit, she arched her back moaning my name. Rising my head, "You are all wet and sweet as honey, Imp." She moaned when I lowered my head feasting on her. Holding her primed cunt open, I slide my tongue in as far as I could and sucked out all the juices. Then replacing my tongue with my finger, I pushed deep until I felt the barrier of her virginity when she winced in pain. I pulled back. I knew I would cause her pain when I fully embedded my cock in her, but not yet.

Fucking her with my one finger and alternated using my tongue or rubbed my thumb over her clit, "Do not cum without permission." I demanded. She was straining to hold back and getting closer to the edge at the same time.

Finally, "Please!" She cried out.

"Yes, now Melissa." When I granted her permission, she exploded. The walls of her cunt pulsed over my finger, I held her legs wide as I went down and lapped up her orgasm, my face and beard were soaked when I came up. Positioning myself, I guided the tip of my cock to her entrance, "Look at me, Imp."

Her beautiful eyes, opened to me, "Mellise Muller, do you come here of your own free will to be mated with me?"

"Yes," She responded.

"And I Prince Murdoc Keithen Sinclair, Prince of Arcadia, and Laird of the Lycan Clan Sinclair take you as my mate and promise to protect you for the rest of our days." When I finished, I slid slowly into her, until I felt the barrier, "Melissa, say my name."

She sensed what I was going to do, but obeyed, "Murdoc," she moaned half with pleasure half in pain as I pushed through taking what would only be mine. She didn't make a sound, just grasped my arms digging her nails into me.

Lowering my face, I kissed her soft at first, but it turned hungry and demanding from both of us as I moved in and out of her. I could feel her body tightening, but I would not let her have control, "Not yet, Imp." I said against her mouth. Thrusting harder, I was seeing how long we both could hold on, when I knew I was at the edge, "Now, Melissa, cum with me." As the walls of her cunt pulsed, I exploded in her throwing my head back and howling.

Flipping her over onto her knees, I grabbed her thick mane of hair and twisted her head to the side, thrusting deep into her core again, my beast surfaced lowering his head, and sinking our fangs into the delicate skin of her neck. "Yes!" she moaned. Biting the inside of my lip I let the drops of blood flow into her body and mingle with hers.

My beast roared at the taste of her blood; then went down for more. Sucking her blood into my mouth it mingled with mine from the wound in my mouth. I felt a sensation like I have never felt before. My beast emerged fully and fucked our mate hard not letting up, we both were stronger than before. She was moaning and lost in the sensations of our joined bodies. Her body shook, and I could see her fingers turn into claws as we both came at the same time, and I howled louder than I ever had, as she screamed out her orgasm, I could see the trees sway it was so strong.

"Murdoc!" she cried.

I came back to my human self, and held onto her, "It's all right. Melissa just breath," She was afraid of her transformation, and I still was not sure of what had happened to me. "Your blood did something to me."

"I felt it too. The spell is broken." She whispered.

We both turned our heads at the sound of running, I jumped up and grabbed her robe covering her naked body with it. As I reached for my jeans, Lucas, Grayson and three of my security crashed through the trees ready to kill any intruders. Raising my hand, "Stop!" I called out.

Lucas and Grayson looked at each other, and both grinned. My security looked confused at the sight before them. "Turn around all of you!" I commanded. Thankfully they all did as I demanded. Reaching down I helped Melissa stand and put on her robe, then I stepped in front of her, putting on my jeans. "You three return to the compound," I ordered.

Lucas and Grayson turned around, "Melissa will be staying with me this evening. And she apologizes for sneaking out of your house, Lucas."

Lucas nodded his acceptance of my apology, "We will talk in the morning." He turned to leave back the way he came.

Grayson stepped forward, "Congratulations, brother," then he bowed his head to Melissa, "Princess." Then he too turned and left.

When I turned around Melissa was looking down at her hands, "How do you feel?" I asked.

She smiled, "A little embarrassed. Does that always happen..." She fluttered her hand in the direction they just left, "They come crashing in?"

"I hope not!" I grinned, as I reached for my boots handing them to her, then I picked her up. Carrying her to Noah's and up the stairs to my room. After I put her down, "I am not done with you, yet." I grinned.

"Good," she smiled.

I stalked over to her, as she backed up to the edge of the bed, dropping my boots and then stripping off her robe. Scooting back on the bed, she spread her legs for me. We spent the rest of the night mating.

Chapter 18

Melissa

Memories of this feeling came flooding back from the time I was a resident, working long hours without stopping. Murdoc and I were up mating until the sun peaked over the eastern horizon. I was sore but felt good. The spell was broken, a surge of power like lightning had struck and coursed into my veins as his blood flowed into me, I became stronger physically. He said that my blood did something to him as well.

When my beast started to surface, it scared me. Even being half Lycan, my beast had never emerged. I guess that is going to be a conversation with Victoria. But for now, I am naked and draped across Murdoc. A hard slap landed on my butt. "Why are you awake and thinking so hard? I can hear every word," Murdoc grumbled.

"I am sorry," stretching up I kissed his chest. Then quieted my mind, falling back to sleep. My dreams were not peaceful, those frighting visions were coming in waves, and I could not stop them. "STOP!" I cried out.

Murdoc came running through the door, "Melissa," taking me into his arms. As he pushed my hair back from my face, "What happened?"

Tears were streaming down my face, "The visions." I was terrified of what I had seen.

Murdoc stood and walked into the bathroom, "Let's get you in a hot bath, and dressed. Then we can talk."

Getting up I reached for my robe and walked into the bathroom. "Murdoc, stay with me." Even though he nodded, he didn't understand that I meant I didn't want him to go back to Scotland without me. I pulled my hair up into a floppy bun on top of my head and dropped my robe, Murdoc's eyes roamed from the top of my head to the tips of my toes. I could see the appreciation of what he was seeing. "Keep looking at me like that, and the water will get cold." I smiled.

He chuckled and nodded in agreement, then held out his hand, helping me in the tub, he sat on the edge as I sunk into the hot water. Sighing with pleasure as the heat engulfed me, I closed my eyes. His fingers ran over the marks on the side of my neck, "You are mine now, Imp. How do you feel?"

"A little sore, but I will be fine." Reaching my hand I touched the marks on my neck, "You said my blood did something to you. What happened?" I asked.

Tilting his head, his eyes were vague, "I felt stronger, more powerful. Even my beast was bigger. Did I hurt you when he emerged?"

"No, I don't think so," I smiled, "I felt like a bolt of lightning went through me. I felt stronger too." Then looking down at my hands in the water, "When my beast started to emerge, it scared me."

"You were thinking about talking to Victoria this morning." He smiled.

"Sorry, I didn't mean to wake you up." He reached over and took a sponge off the side of the tub. "And I will talk to her, about meditating."

Soaping it up, "Lean forward, this bath is taking forever." He washed my back and then started to run his hand down my breasts he dropped the sponge in the water, "You had better finish up yourself."

"Maybe so," I took the sponge, a small knock came sounded on the bedroom door, and Murdoc got up, to answer the intrusion. A moment later he came back in with a bag, "Lucas, wants to talk when you are done and have eaten." He laid the bag on the counter, "Some clothes, you can't be running around in just your robe." He grinned.

I finished up and went downstairs to find Samantha with a plate of food and a coffee brewing in the pot. "Lucas and Murdoc are at our house talking about security for you now that you are …" She stopped and stepped up to me wrapping her arms around me in a hug, "Congratulations, Your Highness."

Rolling my eyes, "I don't think I will ever get used to that. Just call me Melissa as before. I guess we are cousins now."

She smiled, "I guess so. Melissa."

"I am sorry I used a spell so you could not hear me leave last night." I laid my hand on top of hers.

Grinning she patted my hand, "It all worked out in the end. I see," she pointed to my neck.

With a big, satisfied grin, "Yes it did." I could not help but turn red and giggled like a schoolgirl, "I had no idea!"

Samantha laughed, "Neither did I when I first mated with Lucas," she admitted.

My laugh stopped when I looked up, "There is a problem," I closed my eyes and found Murdoc until I could see him, "Murdoc is furious over something one of his security said."

"You can see him, even on the other end of the compound," Samantha asked in wonder.

"Yes," I answered still focused on Murdoc, he turned around toward Noah's, *"Stop it, Imp."* I heard him order me.

Opening my eyes, I looked at Samantha, "He knows I was watching him." I took a deep breath and finished eating. "Thank you for breakfast, I was famished."

Samantha smiled, then tilted her head, "Is it only Murdoc you can see and hear with your mind?

With a shrug, "I don't know, I have never tried with anyone else." And that made me think for a moment. Looking into Samantha's eyes, I thought, *"Can you hear me?"*

Her eyes widened, and she looked intently at me for a moment before speaking, "I could hear you, but not answer you."

Standing I washed up the dishes as Samantha dried and put them away, "I can't stand leaving a mess."

We walked over to her house, and Lucas handed her Aileen when we entered. "I think she is hungry, and I can't do anything about that." He grinned.

I laid my hand on the baby's head, "She isn't hungry..." I lowered my head, "She was missing you." I smiled up at Samantha.

"You can hear our daughter?" Lucas asked. "She is only a few months old and hasn't spoken yet."

As soon as Samantha took her daughter in her arms, she stopped fussing. "She has not learned to form the words yet, but she can think them." Samantha cooed at her daughter and took her upstairs.

Lucas ushered me into his office, "Murdoc is at the training fields, I can send a recruit down to get him."

"No need," I looked out the window of his office, "*Murdoc, I am at Lucas',*" I called out to him, turning my attention back to Lucas I heard Murdoc, *"I'm on the way."* Smiling, "He will be here in a minute."

Lucas shook his head, smiling, "I remember my grandparents talking to one another with their minds." He stood when there was a knock on the door.

Murdoc was covered in dirt from head to toe, "Sorry, I had to bash a couple of heads." He grinned. "I think I have a few of my men I would like to send here, with your permission of course."

Lucas looked Murdoc up and down, "Take your boots off, or you will have Samantha to answer too," he grunted, then added, "As long as the Order does not mind, we will train any of your, men."

Murdoc took his boots off and laid them outside the front door, then refused a chair that Lucas offered him, "I am too dirty to sit, but thank you." Then he leaned down and kissed the top of my head. Stepping to the side, he leaned against the door frame.

Lucas, smiled, "I am sorry if this embarrasses you, Melissa." Sighing, "You two made quite a noise when you came together, last night."

Murdoc grunted, and I lowered my head and blushed, "The spell was lifted," was all I could offer him.

Lucas looked up at Murdoc and then at me, "You read some of my grandmother's journal?"

Nodding, "I did. She said that her mother had fallen in love with the man she was telling his future to, and when she had a vision of him marrying another she stopped." Looking up at Murdoc, "That is the main reason he killed her."

"Anything else?" Murdoc asked.

"She said that eventually, she started to share her visions with Callen, your grandfather. She said it was a burden that had been lifted. Except one," turning my attention back to

Lucas, "She saw your Uncle Patrick's death, and wrote that it would crush him if he knew." I looked out the window again, "Something is wrong at the training fields." I uttered.

Just then there was shouting, Lucas and Murdoc both ran out the door, "Stay here!" Murdoc ordered, "Keep Samantha and the young in the house." Lucas called out at the same time.

Samantha came down the stairs, "What's happening?"

I closed my eyes, "Someone was hurt," closing my eyes, I focused on the training fields, *"Do you need me to come and see if I can help?"* I called out to Murdoc.

"No, Jackson is here. Stay there, Imp." He ordered back. Samantha moved toward the front door, I raised my hand, "No, Samantha. Lucas said to keep you and the babies here."

She tried to pull the door open, and it would not budge. "Are you doing this?"

I just nodded, "Lucas and Murdoc are not harmed." Turning my eyes to her, "I will let them in when they return, please go back upstairs."

Samantha did as I ordered, and I kept the doors closed with my mind until I heard Murdoc in my mind, *"We are on the way back."* I didn't respond, I could tell he was furious, I just released my hold on the doors and walked upstairs to tell Samantha they were coming back.

When I came down, "I am sorry." I whispered as I walked up to Murdoc, wrapping my arms around him. "How is he?"

He took a deep breath, "He will heal," He closed his eyes, "What a fucking mess," grumbling. "I will take him back with me tomorrow." His eyes were red and glowing, "Lucas, this means there is either a traitor in my men or your recruits, maybe both."

Shocked, I tried to pull away from Murdoc, "They know!" Looking up at Murdoc, "They know we broke the spell."

"Yes," He answered looking down at me, taking my hand, "Let's talk." We walked into Lucas' office, "Sit down, and close your eyes."

I did as he asked, "Think back, and tell me what the one that killed your parents looked like."

He had knelt in front of me and was holding my hands. Taking deep breaths, my mind went back to the night, "I had walking back from my car. I stopped about a half block away from the house. My mother screamed." Taking another breath, "My father roared, then there was nothing." Opening my eyes, I looked at Murdoc, and he nodded. "Esmee called out to me, saying they were dead, and I needed to leave. But I didn't, I could not move. I stood behind a tree and watched."

Lucas had moved into the study and was taking notes as I talked. "Flames started to shoot out the upstairs windows, my old room, then my parent's room." Looking down at Murdoc's large hands covering mine, "He came out, and looked around, smelling the air."

Closing my eyes again, "He is tall, not as tall as you, maybe older, but not much." Concentrating on the past, "When his head turned toward me, I could see a scar on his face." Looking at Murdoc, "How is that so, Lycan's don't scar."

Growling, "They do if they are injured by another being." Turning his head, "I know who is behind this."

Grayson and Victoria had walked in, "MacDonald." Grayson growled at the same time Murdoc did.

I had to get it out, "Do you have a dungeon at your home?"

Murdoc was shocked at the question, "No, why?"

A tear slipped down my cheek, "I have seen you chained to a wall, there are bars, across the room, and it is damp and dirty. You are in danger, Murdoc. He will try to kill you." I reached out my hand and stoked his face trailing my fingers through his beard. "There is an old battle axe near you, but you can't get to it."

Murdoc had raised his hand and was cupping my face, "MacDonald does not have an axe to my knowledge."

Grayson folded his arms across his chest, "But you do. In the old armory hall. One of grandfather's old axes."

Lucas spoke up, "Melissa, why don't you go in the kitchen with Samantha and Victoria." It was a nicely worded command.

"He does know I can hear you thinking?" I rolled my eyes as I stood and did as I was told. Murdoc stood with me, smiling, and shook his head.

Lucas watched me leave, "What do you intend on doing about MacDonald?"

"I am going to kill him." I heard Mudoc say.

After that, I heard the front door close, sighing, I looked up at Samantha, "I am sorry, I was just doing what Lucas said."

Victoria looked to Samantha and then me, "What did you do?"

Samantha sighed, "I know, but it was just a shock that you could do that with your mind." Then she looked at Victoria, "She held the doors closed so I could not leave."

"With your mind?" Victoria asked. When I nodded, "Wow!"

Samantha, stood and moved to the refrigerator, "Okay what are we going to make those three for dinner?" Smiling over her shoulder, "I am assuming that you all are staying for dinner." It was a statement and not a question.

"I will help, but I have never been a cook. Microwaved and ate takeout my way through college." I stood and offered, "But I am at your command, Ms. General."

Victoria came over to help, and soon we had pots and pans on the stove, and I was chopping vegetables, for Samantha. "You are a pro at chopping!" she giggled.

Twirling a knife around my fingers, "I am a surgeon." Grinning.

"So, this isn't one of your powers?" Victoria asked.

"No, I studied long and hard to become a general surgeon." I thought for a moment, "I guess that life is over." That thought made me a little sad.

"Can you hear Murdoc and Lucas?" Samantha asked.

"I hadn't been listening," I replied.

We continued to chat, and I helped cook until Murdoc, Lucas, and Grayson came back. "Just in time for dinner, Lucas call the others please," Samanta called out. The first thing I noticed was Murdoc had showered and was now dressed in a white T-shirt and jeans that hugged him perfectly.

"Stop! You are going to make me hard." Murdoc ordered, I turned my head and blushed. Lucas laughed shaking his head.

Levi, Noah, Jackson, and Wyatt all came in and we sat around the large dining table. Chatting and eating as one large family. "Is this what dinner is like at your home?" I whispered to Murdoc.

He shook his head, "Most of the time it is just me." Then he shrugged, "But Airma has been staying for about a week or so."

"Who's Amira?" I asked.

Grayson hears, "Amira is our niece." He smiled, "Our sister Beatrice's daughter, or now oldest daughter."

"You have a sister?" I looked at Murdoc and then Grayson.

Murdoc smiled, "I guess we need to learn a lot more about each other."

A knock came on the front door, Levi held up his hand when Lucas started to stand, "That is probably Patrick. He got back this evening."

"Tell him to come in and eat," Samantha called out. Standing, "I will get another plate."

A tall and handsome Lycan came in, with black hair and piercing eyes. Levi introduced Murdoc and then me. "Your Highness" he bowed to Murdoc, then turned to me, "Your Highness." He smiled. Murdoc growled.

Samantha laughed, "Patrick quit playing before Murdoc tears your head off."

When dinner was finished, I helped with the dishes, Murdoc came and wrapped his arms around my waist, "Go pack a bag for the night. You are staying with me." He whispered in my ear.

Chapter 19

Murdoc

Melissa had another hot bath and was now gloriously nude wrapped up in my arms. I was worried about leaving her here, but there were more issues with taking her with me. I listened to her when she told me about her visions, and that I was in danger, but I was not going to take a chance with her life. The thought that I could have gotten her pregnant last night thrilled and terrified me at the same time.

She was running her fingers through the hair on my chest, and I knew she was thinking, but I could not hear her, "You are blocking me out. Why?"

"Not just you, I am trying to block out the visions too." She said, "I know you have to leave tomorrow, and I am worried about you. But there is one thing that is keeping me from being terrified." She had propped her head on her hands and was looking me in the eyes.

"What is that?" I asked rubbing her bare ass.

"Another vision I saw," she smiled.

"Tell me," I ordered.

"Is there a field with flowers..." she started.

"Yes, to the west of the house," I told her.

"We are there, watching our children run and play." She smiled brightly.

"Children? More than one?" I asked. She just nodded and raised four fingers on her hand.

Chuckling, "Four!" I pushed her over on her back, "Well then I need to get busy starting this pack of ours." Before I moved to slide into her, "Are you still sore?"

She trailed her fingers down my chest until she reached my throbbing cock, "Yes, but I want you to fill me up." She smiled.

Lowering my head to kiss her, "Imp," I growled as I slid into her slick entrance.

We mated for some time before Melissa finally fell asleep on my chest. I held on to her, almost as if my life depended on her. Shaking my head, four pups, by all the gods, I never thought I could be so blessed in my long life.

Melissa moaned in her sleep, and I whispered to her until she quieted. Closing my eyes, I had to deal with this threat so that she could sleep peacefully, in these short few days, Melissa had become my world.

When the streaks of the sun came in through the windows, I got up. "Is it time for you to leave?" Melissa's voice was groggy and sleep-filled.

"Not yet, this afternoon," I said. "I have some things I need to do before I leave," I answered. Melissa moved to get out of bed, "Where are you going?"

"I am going to get dressed and check on your security that got hurt yesterday." She smiled, "But before that, I am going to clean up this room, and wash the sheets for Noah." Now folding her arms over her bare breasts, "I refuse to leave him to clean up after us."

When she turned to walk into the bathroom, I smacked her ass. She laughed as she ran through the door. When the shower turned on, I was tempted to climb in with her. When this is all over, I will keep her nude twenty-four-seven, I thought as I walked out of the bedroom.

I didn't see Melissa for some hours, and it was getting close to the time for me to leave. She walked out of Samantha's, her head was down, and I could tell she was upset. Walking up to her, I lifted her face, "What is all this? You were acting fine this morning." I asked.

"I was pretending this morning." She tried to smile.

Taking her hand, I pulled her away from the awaiting SUVs. "Kiss me goodbye, Imp," I ordered.

She wound her hands around my neck, "Take me with you." She pleaded.

Kissing her nose, "No, you are safer here," then sterner, "Obey me." I growled.

Tears welled up in her eyes, "Yes, Your Highness." She whispered and pulled my face down to her, licking my lips with the tip of her tongue.

Growling deep I pulled her tighter, deepening the kiss. We stayed entangled for several long minutes. When I heard a cough behind me. Pulling myself away, "Brother, you need better timing."

"Better?" he chuckled. "I think my timing is perfect, you were about to take your Princess out to the woods."

Grayson was right, if I had held Melissa much longer, I would have pulled her out to the lake and stayed until tomorrow. Releasing my hold, I took her hand and walked to Grayson, placing her hand in his, "I am trusting you brother to protect her." My eyes glowed, I was not joking.

Looking up I saw Lucas by the SUV waiting for me, "You too, Lucas. Keep her safe! It is my command."

Lucas bowed his head, "It will be done, Your Highness."

Turning I looked at Melissa, *"Imp, you will trust them to keep you safe."* I spoke the words to her mind.

"I will, Your Highness," she responded.

Walking over to the SUV, I got in the back, the three security that was coming with me were in the second vehicle, Lucas rode in the front seat, Patrick Sheen was in the back with me, and Levi drove us to the airport. Closing my eyes, I could feel Melissa watching me. I didn't reprimand her, I knew of her fear, that I was walking into danger.

Patrick knew the plan, but my security didn't. And that was for the best.

When we got to the airport, there were two planes on the tarmac, Patrick pulled a pistol and shot my security with tranquilizing darts. They fell to the ground.

After we tied them up and secured them in the cargo hold of the first plane. We waited.

Chapter 20

Melissa

Grayson didn't let go of my hand as we watched the SUVs leave the compound. Catching movement, I watched as Wyatt, Noah, and Jackson walked up behind the remaining security that Murdoc left to protect me and injected them in the neck. After they fell to the ground, they pulled them to the mine entrance, Grayson turned, "Go and pack, quickly. We are leaving in thirty minutes." I smiled and turned running to Samantha's.

"Samantha, I am going with Murdoc," I called out when I opened the front door, then I saw the car seats and bags packed at the door.

Confused, "Go and hurry," she called out from the kitchen.

It didn't take me any time to pack up, since I really had not unpacked much, most of my clothes were still in suitcases. Bringing my bags down, Samantha and Victoria each had one of her babes carrying them out to awaiting SUVs. A recruit came and took my bags out to the waiting SUVs. Still confused, *"Murdoc, what is going on?"* I called out to him. He didn't respond, and his mind was closed to me, or maybe it was the distance.

Grayson came up and took my hand leading me to the front SUV, getting in, the back with Victoria, and in the front were Wyatt, and Grayson driving. The second SUV had Samantha with the babies, Noah, and Jackson. Murdoc was not going alone. We drove for an hour to get to the airport, I jumped out as soon as Grayson put the car in park and ran to Murdoc. Catching me when I flung myself at him, "Imp, you are not coming with me," he said. "You three with the babies are going to Fergus' where all of you will be safe. He is expecting you, and Gerard is going to heal."

I looked over my shoulder, to see Noah and Levi loading our bags into a second plane. "I don't understand."

"When, Gerard, woke up from being hurt, he was able to tell us some of what happened." He started to explain, "Lucas, Grayson, and I decided to take MacDonald by surprise." Holding his fingers to my lips, "But I was not going to leave you or them," he motioned to Samantha and Victoria, "in harm's way. They had orders to kill all of you."

My heart sank, as a tear fell at the thought that this MacDonald hated me so much that he would kill innocent pups. "Murdoc, don't close your mind to me, let me see what is happening, please."

He nodded, knowing that I would fight to go with them if he didn't agree. Out of the corner of my eye, I saw Grayson kissing Victoria, and Lucas kissing Samantha and his young. Stretching up on my tiptoes, "Remember, we have a pack of pups to make yet." I gave him a weak smile and kissed him before turning and following Samantha and Victoria to the plane.

Once inside, I closed my eyes and found Murdoc seated in his plane. I saw him shake his head, and smile. *"Imp,"* I heard him.

We took off before they did, but I still could see him even as the distance grew. A few moments later, they were also in the air following not far behind us. The two planes were close as they could risk until we got to the border of Scotland, Murdoc's plane started its descent, *"We are going to Glasgow to meet with the High Council and the head of the Order of Arcadia."* Murdoc explained.

I nodded, and even though he could not see me, we remained in the air for another hour before we landed on a private airstrip. When the door opened, Fergus Samantha's father walked into the cabin. "Well, I see I am going to have a house full." He grinned and rubbed his hands together, first greeting Samantha with a hug and his grandbabies. Then he walked up to Victoria, hugging her. Then when he approached me, he bowed, "Your Highness, welcome to my home."

"Thank you so much for taking us in." I shook his outstretched hand, then I folded my arms around him, hugging him.

Patting my back, "They will be fine, my dear. Not to worry." He whispered.

I moved to the side, "Gerard was hurt yesterday, I have checked his vitals, and he is healing, but may need some help down the stairs."

Fergus smiled, "You are a doctor I hear; I have men waiting to help him and get him comfortable so he can heal." He turned and took my arm, "Now let's get you home, I have a feast waiting for all of you."

Walking me down the stairs of the plane, I looked back to Samantha, "You should be escorting your daughter, not me." I whispered.

He just patted my hand, "You my dear are a Princess of Arcadia. You will always be treated with respect. Samantha understands." We got to an SUV, and he opened the back door for me, "I will see you at the house." Then Victoria slid into the other side of the SUV with me.

The drive was not long, Victoria leaned over, "Wait until you see the inside of this house," she made quotation signs with her fingers.

Pulling up, it looked like an old English manor I had seen in movies, then when the front doors were open, I looked up and around, "Oh my gods!" I muttered.

"Exactly," Victoria said. "I was here several months ago, Grayson was hurt. And I felt like I fell down the rabbit hole in Wonderland."

We were escorted up to the second floor and shown to our rooms. I was awe-struck by the wealth that displayed ancient paintings that went back hundreds of years. My room was decorated in a variety of shades of yellow, it was calming and soothing. I walked over to the bed and sat on the side, concentrating on Murdoc. I could see him in a room seated at a table, closing my eyes, and after a few deep breaths, I could hear what was being said.

"Your Highness, you are going on the word of your female that your commander is the Lycan that killed her parents." One of the elders spoke.

"Melissa is not ordinary; she is the last descendant of Esmee," Murdoc replies.

"Esmee died hundreds of years ago, her descendants have all died out." Another said.

"Really, and how would you know where and how Esmée's descendants have perished?" Murdoc's eyes glowed.

Grayson laid his hand on Murdoc's shoulder, "Is she with you brother?" he uttered. Murdoc nodded.

Murdoc closed his eyes, "You will have to prove your powers, Imp." He said aloud for all the elders to hear.

I looked at the one that questioned my being Esmée's descendant. There were papers under his hands, concentrating. I lifted his hands and with a wave of my hand, the papers flew across the room.

Shocked the elders stood, the one that said everyone in my family line had perished, his eyes glowed, and he growled, "Where is the witch?" He looked around the room, then I saw a tattoo, it was familiar.

Breaking my connection with Murdoc, I concentrated on the night my parents died, there on his neck, the same tattoo. Quickly I went back to Murdoc, *"The elder, he has the same tattoo as the one that killed my parents!"*

Lucas, Grayson, and the others were standing around the elder, he was being injected in the arm. "My man, you ordered to have killed, told us that MacDonald was not the head of the Lycans that have hunted witches," Murdoc growled.

Chaos ensued in the room, the elders were all talking at once, but I smiled, as the elder was taken away, "My lords, I need to clean out the nest of these despicable Lycans from my clan. MacDonald is from a wealthy and ancient Lycan family. Unless they are also behind these deaths, I have no problem with them." He looked at one of the elders that was about to speak, "I do not wish to start any wars in our world either, but I will not have my mate and future mother of my young hunted down." Then grinning, "She could be carrying my heir as we speak."

The remaining elders gathered and talked among themselves. Then one spoke, "Your Highness, we agree that hunting to kill any being in our world is despicable. We will order a unit of the Knights of Arcadia to be sent to the MacDonald clan and investigate further."

Lucas looked at Grayson, and shrugged, "Furthermore, we will not take any action against you, in the event of cleaning out the vermin in your clan. We wish you luck."

Stepping back for a moment, he turned back around, "And our congratulations on your recent mating. May she bless you many young."

"Am I just a broodmare?" I said to him. *"Honestly, I am a general surgeon. And damn proud of it."*

Murdoc lowered his head so that the council could not see him smiling. *"Imp. Are you done now?"*

Sighing, *"Yes, but seriously."* Taking a couple of calming breaths, *"When do you leave to trap MacDonald? I could help, my powers are growing."*

"You are not to try to come!" He growled in my head. *"Say the words, Imp!"*

"Yes, Your Highness," I muttered. A knock came on my bed-room door.

Victoria looked in, "Dinner is ready, Melissa."

Nodding, *"Dinner is ready, but I am not hungry."* I thought, knowing that Murdoc was listening.

"Go, you are a Princess of Arcadia." He responded, then closed his mind to me.

Chapter 21

Murdoc

We were sitting in Liam's house just outside of Glasgow. Coming up and slapping me on the back, "You would have to mate with the most powerful witch in our world." He laughed.

Then nodding to Lucas, "Brother. Where are my niece and nephew?"

Lucas grunted, "Safe, I will bring them to see you when this is finished." Liam made his rounds to the others greeting them.

Sitting down to a feast, "I would like to accompany you tomorrow." Liam announced.

"This is not your fight," I countered.

"Ahh, but it is, we are Princes of Arcadia, and we must protect the Lycaon name. I have spoken to the others, and they all agree, we need to deal with this problem promptly." His eagerness was evident.

I looked over to Lucas, Liam was his brother, hopefully, he could help talk him out of this. Lucas got the hint. "When was the last time you held a sword? Or fought?"

Liam was not deterred, "Daily."

Lucas stood, "We train daily, brother." He motioned to the others in the room, "I cannot allow you, to go with us. I must think of your safety."

Liam, stood and grew at least three inches, "You will not allow it? Lucas, please remember who I am."

Lucas stood but did not allow his beast to surface, "You are a Prince of Arcadia, but first you are my younger brother."

Liam sighed and came back to his human side shaking his head, "You always pull the little brother card."

Lucas slapped his brother on the back, "Because it works."

The hours flew past, and none of us were able to sleep. I walked out into the courtyard and opened my mind to Melissa. *"Imp,"* I whispered, not wanting to wake her if she was asleep.

"Murdoc, thank the gods," She whispered back.

"Why are you whispering in my head?" I asked.

"I don't know. Where are you?" she asked.

"See for yourself," I said. The breeze picked up and a warmth came over me, she was seeing what I was. *"We are at Liam's, Lucas' brother."* I clarified.

"I can see the lights of the city." She was tired I could tell.

"Go to sleep, we are leaving early. I may need your help, but from where you are." I instructed. *"Understand, Imp."*

"Yes, Your Highness." She whispered.

"Say my name," I ordered.

"Murdoc," she moaned.

"Tomorrow, Melissa. Tomorrow this will all be over." Murdoc said, *"Good night."*

Chapter 22

Melissa

"The best-laid plans of mice and men often go awry."
An Adapted line from: "To a Mouse," by Robert Burns

My mind was scattered, I couldn't focus on anything. *"Murdoc!"* I screamed.

"Imp, they have me." His voice sounded just as groggy as I felt.

"Me too. I don't know where I am." I had to keep talking to him, it was the only way I could stay calm, and wake up. *"Esmee, please help me."* Calling out to her.

"I am here," Thank the gods she answered. *"Stay calm and breath, you are close to him, and together your powers are stronger."*

"Murdoc, did you hear her?" I asked.

"Yes," he sounded weak.

"Stay with me," I said, *"Open your eyes,"* coaxing him. *"I need to see where you are."* I could tell he was struggling to open his eyes, but once he did, I could see the damp cell I had seen him in my visions. *"Good, now tell me what do you want first? A boy or a girl?"*

His breathing was calming down, *"You want to talk about that now?"*

"No, I am trying to calm you down and focus. Look around I need to see everything." He did as I asked, there against the wall was the axe.

"Is that your grandfather's axe?" I asked.

"Yes," he answered. *"Someone is near, I can hear them."*

"Me too, do not close your mind." I reminded him. *"There against the wall is that a rat?"*

He looked, a rat was scurrying along the edge of the wall. *"I am going to leave you, just for a minute."* Concentrating on the rodent and was able to connect with him. Getting him to move to the bars, I could see what was happening outside of the cell. Two of his security were there, talking. "When is MacDonald coming?"

"Patience, he is busy with the niece."

"He said we could have her when this is finished. Where is he taking her?"

"Nowhere, he was locking her in her room."

"AGH! There is a rat!" He reached down to grab him; I was still connected. "Fuck he bit me! He yelled and tossed the rat back down to the ground; I was able to get back to Murdoc.

"What happened, are you all right? Murdoc asked me.

"Yes, they are waiting for MacDonald to come," I answered him. *"He has your niece locked up in her room."*

"Where are the others, or did they just take me?" He asked.

"Is she awake?" I let Murdoc hear what was going on around me. My head had been covered, and the hood was lifted when he spoke. I looked up into the eyes of the one that had killed my parents.

"Good, you're awake!" He grinned.

"MacDonald, you will not be able to kill me so easily," I growled. "I am stronger than my mother."

MacDonald was taken aback by the fact I knew his name and only showed it for a second before he schooled his expression back to one of indifference. "I have you and the Prince." He grinned, "You will stand against that tree so I can do away with you, or you will watch as I kill him." He grinned, "And he will do as I ask, or I will kill his niece." Shrugging his shoulders, "See, you are not as smart as you think Doctor."

I was on my knees looking at the tree that MacDonald's men brought wood to pile around the base. Keeping my eyes trained on MacDonald, I focused on Lucas, we needed help. "Lucas, MacDonald has Murdoc and me. Please come quick."

Not relying on if Lucas had heard me or not, it was time I took matters to myself.

Focusing on the robes that were around my wrists, I moved them, slowly untying my hands. MacDonald and his men were busy talking and were not paying any attention to me. Then they walked off. I knew he wanted to be here when they set me on fire, so I had time. And now only one of his men to deal with. *"Esmee help me, tell me what to do,"*

"Your mind and your words are your greatest power," she said, *"Beings, animals, and objects will obey your every command. Use them."*

Looking at the tree where they had gathered the wood, "Go back to where they found you." Then watching the wood rose and moved back into the forest.

"What the hell!" The guard turned to raise his sword.

I lifted my hand, "Stop!" yelling. He froze, unable to move, "Drop it!" I commanded his hand and released his sword and it fell to the ground.

Noah came from behind a tree, holding his sword, "I have him, Your Highness." Then Wyatt came and offered me his hand.

"The others, I didn't see what happened to Samantha and Victoria," tears streamed down my face, "Please tell me they are unharmed."

"They are fine," Wyatt said, as soon as we realized Murdoc was missing, we split up," he answered me.

Nodding, "They have his niece locked in her room," I told them, and a feeling of dread came over me. "I have to get to Murdoc."

Wyatt explained, "Grayson and Patrick are searching for her in the house. They will find her." I only heard half of what he said, as I ran in the direction my heart was telling me.

Chapter 23

Murdoc

Melissa was out in the woods; I could see and hear everything that was happening. I could even feel the ropes come loose behind her back as MacDonald left her there with only one guard. MacDonald stepped into my sight, and my connection with her was lost. He wasn't alone, Isabelle was there too.

"What do you think of your mate, Isabelle?" MacDonald sneered. "I told you, I would arrange it, so you mated with him."

"He doesn't look that impressive to me, Father," she grumbled. "I would prefer one of the others, maybe Prince Cane."

It took all my effort to not roll my eyes at this silly chit of a female. "I am already mated." Speaking to MacDonald, "Melissa is free."

"Impossible, I left her tied and she is ready to die to save your life." He thought that Melissa agreed to his demands.

Shaking my head, "You don't know a thing about my mate," I chuckled, "Not only is she beautiful, but she is powerful. I am telling the truth; she is free of her bounds."

Isabelle stepped forward and slapped my face, "You lie!" she screamed. Power was surging through me, Melissa was near.

Lowering and tilting my head, *"I can feel you, Imp."* Then I felt the lock on the chains open, I was free.

MacDonald saw that I was liberated from the chains, "How did you release yourself?"

"I didn't," pointing to the now open cage door, "Melissa released me." Slowly standing, I reached over and grasped the hilt of my grandfather's axe. "You are going to have to pay for your crimes."

Isabelle turned and ran. MacDonald let his beast surface, "You were never strong enough to wield that." He pointed to the axe in my hand.

My beast was also emerging, "I am now," I growled.

MacDonald lunged at me with his sword, moving to my right I deflected the blow and then stepped back. This axe was heavy, and I had not held it for nearly two hundred years. Taking a deep breath, Melissa came into my view standing at the cage door. I saw Wyatt behind her holding her back. "Traitor!" I yelled, swinging the axe from the right to left, just grazing his shirt. My eyes flashed! "You will die today, MacDonald!"

MacDonald jumped back from my blow, and glanced behind him, he snarled at Melissa, "The witch will die!" Throwing back his head he howled long and deep, his men came scurrying out like rats from the other end of the cave we were in. Wyatt pushed Melissa behind him when I heard Grayson howl and advanced on the four that were trying to surround Wyatt and Melissa.

MacDonald's men were not a match for them, and soon, they were either dead or severely wounded. Melissa's eyes were pure blue as she kept her eyes on me, not watching what was happening around her. Grayson and Wyatt took up positions on each side of her, protecting her, Grayson nodded. "Finish it, brother," He growled out.

Stepping close to MacDonald again, I brought my axe up and then down, causing a gash from the right side of his chest to the left, blood poured out of the wound, but it was not enough to kill him, more of his men came running into the cave, Grayson and Wyatt put Melissa between them, "Burn the witch!" MacDonald screamed. I saw one with a glass bottle of something that had a wick at the top, he lit the wick and threw it at Melissa.

"NO!" I yelled and dropped my axe, running to move her.

MacDonald grabbed the axe and backed up throwing it over his head, the impact on my chest was enormous, and I stumbled back. Shocked by the blow, I heard Melissa scream, throwing her hand toward MacDonald, the bottle that was intended for her flew through the cage bars, and crashed on the ground at MacDonald's feet. Her hair was blowing around, but there was no wind, "Burn!" she screamed, her eyes glowing a deep blue.

MacDonald was engulfed in flames, screaming as he burned, she ran to me, Grayson looked at me, with our grandfather's axe in my chest, I nodded, and he swung his sword. MacDonald's head dropped to the ground and rolled across the cage.

Melissa was yelling orders, to get me into the house. "Don't take it out, I have to ...." Those were the last words I heard; everything went black.

Chapter 24

"Don't die, don't die," I chanted over and over, as Grayson and Wyatt carried Murdoc toward the house trying not to shift the axe in his chest. There was a room with medical equipment in one of the outbuildings. They laid him out on the table, and I got to work.

Slowly I cut his shirt away from the blade of the axe to see how deep it was in. So close to his heart, Lycan or not, this was serious. Grayson helped hold his brother down as I found a scalpel and began to cut. Tears were streaming down my face, and I had to wipe them away with my sleeve several times so that I could see what I was doing.

Grayson called orders over his shoulder at Wyatt and Noah, "Gather everyone in the great hall, and start questioning them. This may not be over yet." Then he laid his hand on top of mine, "Breath sister, you can do this."

Calling me sister stunned me, and I looked up and smiled. "I can," then I turned my face back down to Murdoc. Slowly and with the precision of my surgical skills, I peeled back his skin and muscle. The axe broke four ribs, stopping just millimeters from his heart. Grayson had to help me pull it free. Once it was out, I held the broken ribs in place as I focused on his healing powers to fuse them back together, each came together as if they had never been damaged. Continuing as I repaired all four of the broken ribs, then pulling the muscles back into place, holding my hand over them, they closed, then his skin. Murdoc's chest looked perfect, there was not a mark on him, even a bruise. The only evidence was my blood-soaked hands, caressing his cheek, "Open your eyes for me, Murdoc," I said.

Slowly, he did. "What happened?" he asked, looking up at his brother, then at me.

Grayson nodded toward me, "She happened."

Murdoc tried to sit up, I placed my hand on his shoulder, "You need to lay still and heal, you lost a lot of blood."

Murdoc looked down at his chest, "The axe was in my chest," turning his eyes to me, "What did you do? Imp." He growled,

Grayson chuckled, "He's fine." Then he turned, calling over his shoulder, "When you are ready, I have everyone gathered in the great hall, and are questioning them. This may not be over."

Melissa crossed her arms over her chest, "I operated on you," she glared. "With Grayson's help, I got the axe out and repaired your ribs."

Murdoc eyes flashed and narrowed when he reached out and held onto my wrist, "How did you repair my ribs?"

"I used my mind to accelerate your healing powers to fuse your ribs back together, then the muscle and skin I had to cut to get the axe out of you," answering, "You are welcome by the way."

His eyes glowed, "You used your powers on me?" growling even as he grinned.

"To heal you, not against you," I answered.

With a quick jerk, I was leaning over him, his left hand came around my neck pulling my face to his, "Say..."

"Murdoc," I moaned and opened my mouth for the kiss I knew was coming. When we came up for air, I laid my head on his chest, "You could have died."

"Never with you around." His arm was around my waist, "I could have lost you, today."

"Gerard was one of them," I said.

"We will find them all," he whispered to my temple. We lay in each other's arms for only a short time, "It is time I got up." Gently he pushed me away, then swung his legs over the side of the table. Looking down at his bare chest, "I think a clean shirt would be a start."

That is when I looked down at myself, "I have your blood all over me." Slumping my shoulders, "All my clothes are at Fergus'."

Murdoc took my hand, "Amira can lend you something."

We walked to the house, I didn't have time to look around as we ascended the stairs, Murdoc pounded on a door, "Amira!"

Patrick opened the door, "Yes," his eyes were red, and glowing. Murdoc grinned, "Think you can handle her?" He offered up his hand.

"Yes," he answered grinning shaking Murdoc's hand.

"Melissa needs to borrow some clothes," Murdoc crossed his arms over his chest.

"Murdoc, don't you dare give him your blessing!" Amira called out from behind Patrick.

"Enough!" Patrick yelled back, "You are mine, deal with it, and stop pouting." I had moved behind Murdoc to hide my laughter.

Murdoc reached out and pulled the door closed, taking my hand again, he pulled me down the hall to a massive bedroom. Shaking his head, he finally chuckled, "He is going to have his hands full with her." When he looked at me still trying to control my giggles, "Imp," he stalked toward me, "You need a bath and a good spanking. I am not sure which one to start with."

I ran to the first closed door when a knock sounded on the door. "What!" Murdoc answered.

Grayson shook his head, "Good to see you back to yourself, brother. Lucas and the others arrived," then he pulled my two suitcases to the door. "Your mate may need these. I have the staff preparing a feast."

"Taking over my household?" Then realizing Grayson was just helping, "We will be down soon." Before Grayson could walk away, "Grayson, about Patrick, we need to talk."

Grayson nodded, "I heard." Turning to walk down the hall-way, "After dinner."

My hair was in desperate need of a wash, but I didn't want to make anyone wait on me, so a messy bun on top of my head was going to have to do. Murdoc came into the bathroom, turning on the water in the shower, "Take off your clothes."

Never in my life was I more than happy to comply, stepping close to him, I trailed my fingers down his chest, then his abdomen, and without being told, I sank to my knees, grasping my fingers around his hard shaft. Pre-cum was at his tip, and licked it off, "May I?"

"Since you are already down there," he grinned, as he threaded his fingers through my hair. Sucking and stroking him, he let me take what I could before his hips started to pump into my mouth, I sat still and let him find his orgasm. When it came, he threw back his head and growled. His semen jutted into my mouth and throat, and I did as he taught me and didn't spill a drop. Licking him clean, I stood. "I will reward you later, Imp." He turned me smacking my ass.

When we got into the shower, he washed me thoroughly, and I was able to wash him in return. As we got dressed, he was quiet, "Melissa, about Amira." He was hesitant to tell me something. Taking a deep breath, "She is prejudiced against humans."

"I'm not human." It was a statement. "But you think she will not like me anyways."

He lowered his head, "Isabelle, MacDonald's daughter, got in her head. I am not sure what she had told her."

Slipping one of my nice blouses on over my head, I stepped to him, "I will win her over." I smiled, laying my hand on his chest.

He looked me straight in the eye, "Without using..."

I didn't let him finish, "I will not use my powers on her." Holding up three fingers, "Girl Scouts Honor."

"What's a girl scout?" He asked.

"I will tell you later. Now, you have guests." I put my arm through his.

"We have guests." He corrected me and walked me down to the great hall.

Chapter 25

Murdoc

Melissa was on my arm, we came down into the great hall. All those in attendance stood and bowed to my Princess. Out of the corner of my eye, I saw Amira try to turn and leave. Not before Patrick grabbed her hand and whispered into her ear. I am pretty sure that Melissa saw the action too, but she took a deep breath and excused herself. She walked over to Amira and embraced her. Then she threaded her arm through Amira's, and I heard her ask her to introduce her to everyone gathered.

Not once did Melissa let go of my niece, and she included her in all the conversations that happened around her. When dinner was to be served, I went to her, "Time to take our place." Offering her my arm, Patrick was right behind me and ushered Amira to her place, sitting beside her.

When were reached the head of the table, I seated Melissa at my right hand, then called out. "My commander as many of you know is no longer here. I will be speaking to any of those who wish to take the position tomorrow, but for tonight," I looked around, "Grayson, brother, please bring your mate and sit beside me."

Grayson led Victoria to sit on my left, and then I lifted my goblet, "As many of you have met my beautiful mate this evening," I looked around for anyone that could be a threat, "I would like to propose a toast to her, your new Princess of Arcadia, and Duchess of the Lycan Clan of Sinclair, Melissa Mueller." Everyone raised their glasses.

I heard Melissa, *"Dr. Mueller."*

Smiling, I looked down into her beautiful eyes, "Excuse me, Dr. Melissa Mueller." Everyone toasted her, and our meal was served. No one interrupted, and no one called out anything hateful to Melissa or Victoria, for which I was thankful.

After dinner was over and the hall had been cleared, I walked over to Melissa, as she talked with Samantha, "You are tired, go up to bed," I ordered.

She smiled and excused herself and left. Two security followed her, "Really? Still?" she growled.

"Until we know the threat has been cleared off our land, yes. Still." I explained then kissed her forehead. "I am going to talk with Lucas and Grayson, I will be up soon."

Now I stood looking out the windows to the immense forest surrounding Sinclair Lycan Holdings. I am still amazed at how much my life has changed since I left to officiate Grayson's mating ceremony. I found my mate, and she was right now up in our bed waiting for me.

Today I could have lost her, and she ended up pulling my grandfather's axe out of my chest. Rubbing where the blade landed, there wasn't a mark, not because I am a Lycan, but because my mate is a powerful witch that healed me, bones and all.

A knock came, interrupting what Lucas was saying, good thing, I had stopped listening. "Enter."

My second in command opened the door, with Isabelle MacDonald grasped by the arm. "Your Highness, we found her at the far western border." He wasn't cruel, but she struggled to get free.

"Thank you," I waved him off, "Isabelle come in," pointing to an empty chair, "Sit," I commanded.

"Are you going to murder me too?" she sneered in my direction. Then she glared at the other two occupants in the room, "Or maybe have one of them, do it?"

"Sit," I ordered again, "I won't tell you again." She flung her hair over her shoulder and glared at me as she sat.

"You could have had me." She muttered.

I wasn't going to take her bait, "You are going to live a long life," I said, "But not here, never here again."

Her eyes widened, "You have no authority over what I do."

She started to stand. "Sit down," I roared. Then I walked over to the door opening it, two older Lycans came in, "Thank you for coming so quickly." Then I turned to Isabelle, "You are correct, I do not have any authority over what you do, but your grandparents do. Do you remember your grandparents?"

"You can't do that to me," she waved her hand toward the older couple. "I am Amira's companion; I work for Beatrice."

She started to stand again, "Amira has found her mate, and Beatrice does not wish for you to return to her home."

Her grandfather came toward her and grasped her arm, "Stand, we are leaving." He bowed to me, "Your Highness, then turning to Lucas and Grayson, "Your Graces."

Isabelle was not done spewing her poison, "Did you know, that one turned a human into a Lycan?" she looked up to her grandfather pointing to Grayson, "A fucking human."

"We all have humans in our family trees." He shook her, "Your mother was human." He growled.

"Victoria is no longer a human" I stated. By now everyone knew the situation that caused Grayson to give his mate Lycan blood.

Shaking her head, "I don't care. To me, she will always be a human, and not worthy of being mated to such a high-ranking Lycan."

This conversation was going nowhere, "Lord and Lady Mac-Donald, I will have one of the security escort you out."

Lady MacDonald had not said a word until now, dabbing her eyes, "I am sorry our son caused you so much trouble, Your Highness. He was such a good boy." She turned and left with her mate and granddaughter.

"Wow, do they have their hands full?" Grayson said at the closed door.

"I have security patrolling all the halls and grounds." I changed the subject, "I want this place cleared out as soon as possible. And I will not take a chance with your mates and young."

Lucas and Grayson stood, "I agree," Lucas said, "We will leave you in the morning. I am taking Samantha and the children to see Liam." Turning to Grayson, "You and Victoria should stay and visit. The rest are going home."

Offering his hand to me, "The Order is sending men tomorrow to help weed out the rest."

"Thank you both." I shook his hand.

After they left, I turned and looked out the window again, this used to be my favorite part of the house. Then I looked up, smiling as I crossed the room, now maybe it's my bedroom.

Epilogue

Melissa

The breeze was cool, even though it was spring. I looked up into Murdoc's face, he was smiling at the antics of our four children, two boys, and twin girls.

The days that followed MacDonald's death, were not easy, Murdoc lost nearly half of his men. Many of them died that day, and some of the traitors that survived, hid in the woods, plotting to get to me. It was almost like living in the Middle Ages, fires burned around the house, and attacks were made nearly nightly.

I didn't use my powers until Murdoc came to me, "Bring them in," he growled.

Closing my eyes, I could see them in the woods, they all looked scared as they turned involuntarily and walked to the house dropping weapons along the way. The men the Order had sent gathered them up and took them away.

We had peace at last, Amira left to go home, still fighting her desires for Patrick, but he didn't give up. Grayson and Lucas came bringing the babies to our official mating ceremony. The other five Princes came too, our house was filled to the rafters. Beatrice, with her mate, and Amira and Patrick. Murdoc insisted only on one thing, that my dress was lapis blue to match my eyes.

The head of the High Council officiated, and the five princes and Grayson stood with Murdoc. My gown was the shade of my eyes, and the moment Murdoc stepped toward the mating circle, his eyes changed. And I knew mine did as well from the reaction on the officiant's face.

Grayson pulled Murdoc aside after the ceremony to tell him Victoria was expecting their first child, she had told me earlier, so I was not surprised when Murdoc mentioned it to me. "What? She is my friend, and I am her doctor. Or was, of course, she told me."

Lowering my head, it was time to confess, "She wants me to come to deliver the baby. But there may be a problem."

Murdoc looked down at me, "What problem?"

"I am expecting too," I whispered.

Murdoc inhaled, "How is it that I cannot smell that you are pregnant? Imp." He growled rolling over and pinning me to the bed with my hands above my head.

"I hid it from you," admitting. I closed my eyes and released the spell.

Murdoc inhaled again. "How long?" he grinned.

"Just a couple of weeks." He moved so he could place his hand on my stomach, then kissed me soundly.

Coming up for a breath, "I guess I can't spank your ass for hiding your condition until you deliver the babe."

I grinned, "As long as I am comfortable and not bleeding, we can continue to mate, in any way you see fit."

Sitting up, he flipped me over his legs and spanked me, rubbing between my legs until I was begging him for release.

Three months later our son was born, Galvin Keithen Sinclair. As soon as I was able, we traveled to the United States so I could deliver Victoria's child. Since she was once human, she did not deliver for six months.

That was five years ago, five wonderful years. I am happy. Look up at Murdoc, "Are you happy?" I asked.

"Very," he said.

The End

From K. L. Stephens

Dear Reader,

I hope you enjoyed Murdoc and Melissa's story as much as I did writing it. These characters came to life for me as I brought them to existence for your enjoyment.

If you loved this book, please leave me a review! I love hearing from my readers.

The Princes of Arcadia series does not end here; Liam's story will be next. I cannot wait to introduce you to him further. Liam will be released in early 2024.

Until then The Lycan Knight series still goes on, Levi's story is to be released in late summer 2023.

Thanks for reading,

K. L. Stephens

About the Author

K L Stephens is the author of paranormal and contemporary romances. She loves to take her readers into the worlds she creates as she writes, where she matched her many flawed heroes, to strong women that come to love them despite their shortcomings.

Her works include The Lycan Knights series, this new series The Princes of Arcadia, and two novella series The Bennett's and Renegades Roadhouse. Her books have received multiple rave reviews from fans across the globe.

Residing in Southeast, Florida with her spoiled Cocker Spaniel and lazy cat. When she is not working you can usually find her cooking, in the garden of her one-acre home, or reading. Her reading interests are as diverse as her writing. From classic, or sweet romances to spicy paranormal shifters and vampires.

The Latest Happenings

Want to keep up with the latest happenings here at my desk:

Sign-up for my NO-SPAM Newsletter
https://www.klstephens.com/newsletterlp

Where to follow me:

BookBub will send you New Release Alerts. Not only that you can check out my latest deals, but also you get an email when I release a new book. So, follow me on BookBub Here:

https://www.bookbub.com/authors/k-l-stephens

My Website
https://www.klstephens.com

Author Page

https://www.facebook.com/KLStephensAuth2

Facebook Fan Club

https://www.facebook.com/groups/klstephensfangroup